For Katherine +

I hope you'll share my

for this remarkable woman

with warm regards —

Max Morath

01/06/10

I LOVE YOU TRULY

A BIOGRAPHICAL NOVEL

BASED ON THE LIFE
OF

CARRIE JACOBS-BOND

by

MAX MORATH

iUniverse, Inc.
New York Bloomington

I LOVE YOU TRULY

A BIOGRAPHICAL NOVEL BASED ON THE LIFE OF

CARRIE JACOBS-BOND, 1862-1946

iUniverse books may be ordered through booksellers or by contacting:

iUniverse
1663 Liberty Drive
Bloomington, IN 47403
www.iuniverse.com
1-800-Authors (1-800-288-4677)

ISBN: 978-0-595-53017-5 (pbk)
ISBN: 978-0-595-63644-0 (cloth)
ISBN: 978-0-595-63071-4 (ebk)

Library of Congress Control Number: 2008941188

Printed in the United States of America

iUniverse rev. date: 12/22/2008

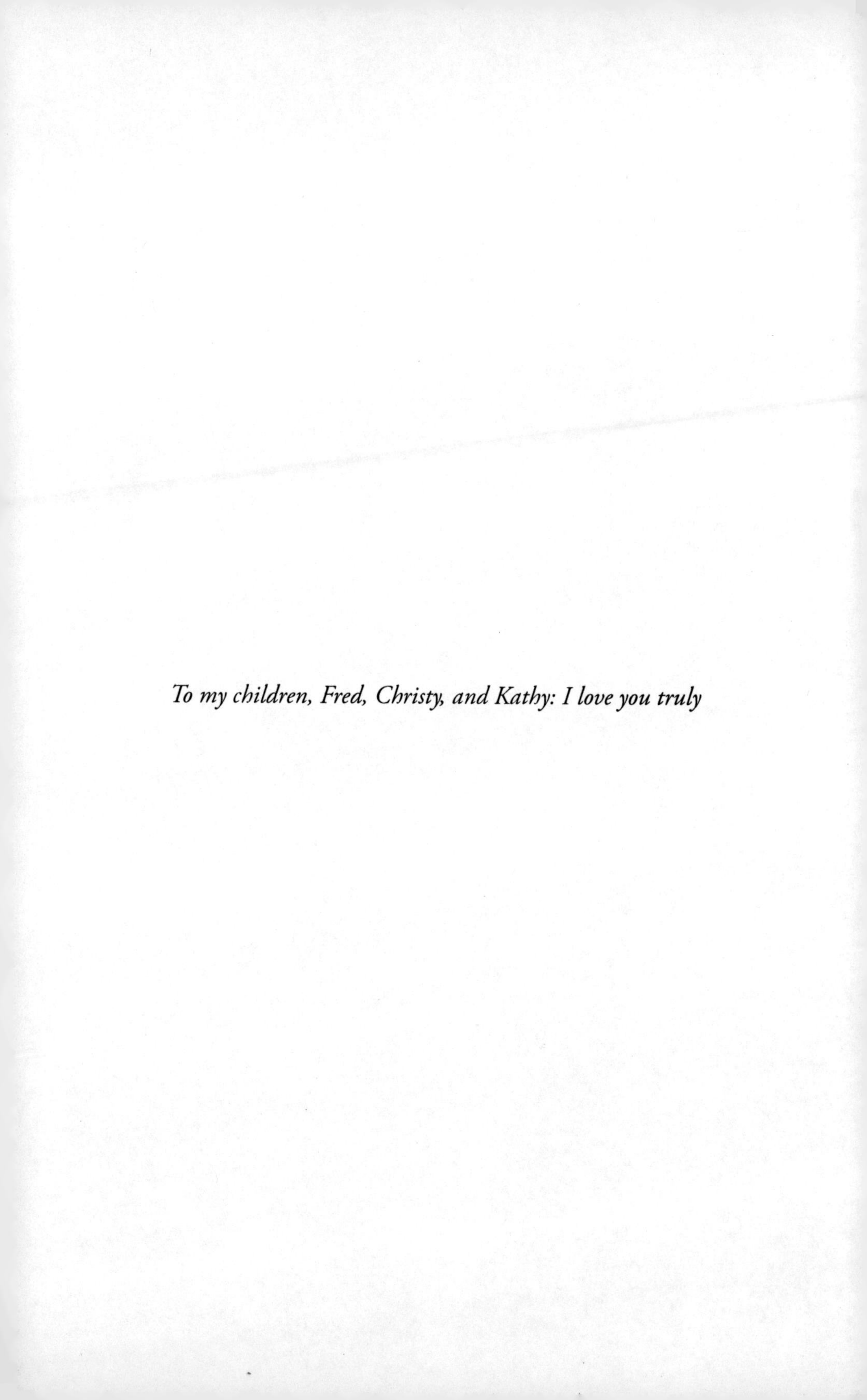

To my children, Fred, Christy, and Kathy: I love you truly

Table of Contents

About the Author

Max Morath occupies a unique space as a spokesman for American life and music. In theatre, broadcasting, publishing, and recording, he has devoted his long career to performing and championing early American popular music and the men and women who produced it. He was among those who spearheaded the ragtime revival of the 1970's with his one-man Off-Broadway show *Turn of the Century.* Other shows followed—*Living a Ragtime Life, Pop Goes the Music*, and *Ragtime and Again*—each new version launched in New York or at Ford's Theater in Washington, DC. In multiple roles as entertainer, pianist, writer, and producer, he logged over 5,000 performances with these shows and other engagements before completing a final tour in 2005. Since then he has devoted all his time to writing and research, with this book a prominent result.

Born in 1926 in Colorado Springs, Morath worked his way through Colorado College as a radio announcer and jazz sideman, graduating with a B.A. in English. A variety of jobs followed: actor, salesman, writer, pianist and television director. Working in melodrama and stock theaters in the West, he developed what would become a lifelong fascination with ragtime and popular song. Graduate studies at Stanford's NBC Radio & Television Institute sharpened his media skills, and in the early 1960's he wrote and performed for PBS twenty-six half-hour programs exploring this music and the colorful America that spawned it. Theatrically-conceived and highly entertaining as well as informative, these shows received wide exposure and critical acclaim throughout the country, leading to a contract with Columbia Records and a nightclub debut at the fabled Blue Angel in New York.

Morath built a parallel career in commercial broadcasting as a writer, narrator, and musician. He was heard for many years with Arthur Godfrey on CBS radio and has appeared on a variety of prime-time television shows. He has also continued to work with Public Broadcasting, on NPR with Marian McPartland's "Piano Jazz" and the Wynton Marsalis series "Making the Music," and on PBS with various specials such as "American Experience:1900" and "Yours for a Song," a retrospective on woman composers of American popular music.

He is the author of *The NPR Curious Listener's Guide to Popular Standards,* and is represented in *The Oxford Companion to Jazz* with the essay "Ragtime Then and Now." He and his wife have published *The Road to Ragtime*, a colorful depiction in photographs and text of the rigors of touring in the America of today. In the theatre, Morath's musical play *Trust Everybody—but Cut the Cards* has been presented in staged readings in New York. It is based on the Mister Dooley essays of the Chicago journalist Finley Peter Dunne and is being readied for further production. He performed in the musical revue *One for the Road*, which he also wrote and co-produced for the Repertory Theater of St. Louis in association with the MUNI Opera Company. That show explored two centuries of America's experience with alcohol and narcotics as reflected in our music and theatre.

Max Morath's recordings are primarily on the Vanguard label. Along with many of his own compositions for piano and voice they include the piano music by Scott Joplin, Eubie Blake, and other icons of the ragtime world, and a selection of rags by woman composers of the early 20th Century. As a singer he has recorded the familiar standards of popular music giants such as Hoagy Carmichael, George & Ira Gershwin, and Irving Berlin, several albums of show tunes with the team of William Bolcom and Joan Morris, and the songs of the legendary African-American performer Bert Williams. As always these projects have been supported by writing and research into the life and times of their subjects.

Morath currently resides in Minnesota with his wife, Diane Fay Skomars, an administrator at the University of Minnesota Duluth (UMD).

Acknowledgments

Through years of research into the life of Carrie Jacobs-Bond, I have been helped and encouraged by many institutions, scholars, and private collectors. Special thanks are due:

Marcia & Harold Bernhardt, Iron River, MI; Phyllis Ruth Bruce, Middletown CT; Dr. Claudia Bushman, Columbia University; Christine Ebert, and especially to Robert DeLand; Beverly Hamer; John Edward Hasse, Smithsonian Institution; Jack Hill (A History of Iron County); Iron County History and Museum Society; Janesville Wisconsin Public Library; Robert Lissauer; Miles & Lynne Maiden; Sandy Marrone; Peter Mintun; Maurice Montgomery; New York Public Library, Lincoln Center; Lisa & Paul Norling; Rock County Historical Society; Loras John Schissel, Library of Congress; Dr. Mark Tucker, Columbia University; thanks also to my eagle-eyed proof reader Christine Ebert; and especially to my wife, Diane Fay Skomars, who combines an ability to spot hidden typos with the grace to offer deep insights about the life and times of this 19th-century woman who has come into our lives.

Max Morath

* * *

Introduction

Carrie Jacobs-Bond was one of the most successful composers and publishers of American popular music of the 20th Century. Her success brought her international fame and a considerable fortune.

As a professional writer and musician I have been attracted to her music since before I can remember. In 1996 I earned a Masters Degree in American Studies at Columbia University, where the title of my thesis was "Three Songs: A Study of Carrie Jacobs-Bond and Her Music." It dealt primarily with her 200 published songs. Among other things, my research produced a seemingly endless list of recordings of her work, revealing that her song *I Love You Truly* is possibly the most frequently recorded tune in all of popular music history. My interest in her "little songs" as she insisted on calling them, gave way to a growing fascination with the remarkable career of Bond herself. It was a storybook life, long and painful, but at the same time romantic and wildly improbable for a woman of her time. Carrie Jacobs-Bond was not a quiet, diffident woman surprised by her success, an image she seemed determined to promote. I found instead a professional woman of passion and determination, for whom life was an unending challenge and adventure. Her success in the man's world of American popular music can only be called a triumph of courage, coupled with a relentless ego. However, her story has for many years been ignored or dismissed on both scholarly and popular levels, due in part to her own lifelong reticence and careless publicity.

Carrie Jacobs-Bond was nearly forty years old before her songs began to attract national attention. She did publish an autobiography, *The Roads of Melody*, but it is largely anecdotal and only moderately helpful. As a result many pages in the story of her life are simply blank. I have filled them in by creating this new autobiography for her. It is a work of fiction, but it is based on years of research. I have explored newspaper files and the archives of the New York Public Library Lincoln Center and the Library of Congress. I have visited her home town and most of her subsequent residences. Actual names and places and dates within reach of my research are faithfully and accurately recorded here. The rest is my studied re-telling of her life. It is a blend of things I know that she did with things I think that she did. There are a few I sentimentally *hope* that she did. She remains a puzzle.

I have no doubt that future scholars will explore her life in foot-noted detail. She was a gifted outsider in a cruelly competitive business, and will surely be documented as a major figure in 20th century American popular culture. I sincerely hope my fanciful attention to the Carrie Jacobs-Bond story will be one of many steps in the rediscovery of this iconic American woman.

Now, in her voice, I humbly begin retelling the story of her life.

Max Morath

* * * *

CHAPTER 1

MY AUTOBIOGRAPHY

In 1927 I wrote an autobiography. It was a volume of soft lies. It was called *The Roads of Melody*, published by D. Appleton of New York and London. It was well-reviewed and enjoyed good sales. The lies were mostly those of omission.

I was sixty-five years old, and had created for myself the public image of a wise and motherly woman. It was not the time to undertake the real story of my life. I was the composer of three of the most enduring love songs of the century—songs about love and friendship—and if you listened closely, about the pain and sweetness of death. They made me wealthy. I owned every note and syllable because I had long since founded my own publishing company, with a catalog of over 200 songs. I was famous and reveled in my fame. If I'm not the woman of simple virtue and courage pictured in *The Roads of Melody*, I can tell you honestly that I've lived a life of hard work, and have overcome a hundred disappointments and mistakes. I brought many of them on myself. As a young woman I was headstrong and selfish. I knew before I was sixteen what I wanted, or thought I wanted, in music and men and money.

Lies by omission? I told you nothing in *The Roads of Melody* about the accident that seared my childhood and has affected my life ever since. When I was seven years old I was horribly burned, scalded actually. Parts of my body were permanently scarred, causing painful breakdowns and hospitalizations ever since, not to mention embarrassed discomfort in my intimate life. Without the constant care of a loving father I doubt I'd have survived. He brought me back to life, and to hope. He died a few months later, when I was eight—"mysteriously," they said. It was 1870. My mother re-married and moved away, leaving me to grow up in a third-floor walk-up at my grandfather's hotel.

I married twice, the first time at eighteen. I had a child, Frederic Jacobs Smith, in a marriage that was damaged from the start. It consumed almost eight ugly years of my life and ended in 1888. In the 224 pages of my other book I dismiss this union with six words: "After seven years we were separated." I was too ashamed to use the word "divorce." Six months later I married the only man I ever truly loved, Dr. Frank Bond. We had seven years together, the happiest of my life. In 1895 Frank Bond died. He was 37. I was 33. I can now acknowledge in these pages that Frank was Frederic's father. You won't see any mention of that in *The Roads of Melody*.

A year after its publication my beloved son took his own life. For many weeks I was sure my grief would overcome my own will to go on living. Obviously it did not. In my closing chapter I explain how I learned to carry on. The unbearable loss of my only child, you see, guided me toward a transformative insight into the nature of death itself. If I needed one more reason impelling me to write again, it was to provide this testimony.

In the eighteen years since I published the autobiography, I have realized my every dream of success as an artist, a composer, a business executive, and gradually, as an independent and acquisitive woman. I have made money undreamed of. I have given much of it away, always quietly and always directly to the needy and to the young, never to charities. My own years in poverty ruled I do it that way. I live quietly today between my two California homes. I have found a life of privacy and freedom that most women could only imagine. I have traveled the world. My friends include movie stars, composers, politicians, and scientists. Through the long years since Frank Bond's death I have enjoyed close and profound friendships with a number of women, some quite famous, others whom I lifted from despondency and want. I have prized as well, lasting ties with many of the young men who have come into my life in search of music and have found companionship as well.

Before I die, I want you to know the truth about my life. Some of it will surprise you, perhaps already has shocked you. I petition your forgiveness in withholding my secrets all these years. I revisit them now in hopes they might provide you a deeper understanding of this American woman, than did the sugar-coated platitudes of her earlier book. In this re-telling of my story I revisit many a chapter in *The Roads of Melody*, sometimes to add, sometimes to subtract from that rather careless narrative. Pain and poverty and death remain essential to my story, but there were also lots of good times and good friends, and I shan't diminish, but will often enlarge upon those memories. Unchanged is the story of a woman born with a mysterious gift of music that brought her unfailing inner strength and happiness. And does to this day.

The title of this new memoir will be the title of my first successful song, *I Love You Truly*. I dedicate it to the memory of my true love Frank Lewis Bond, and to all of you, for singing my songs for so many years. I've been helped every step of the way by my dear, dear Jaime Palmer, who came into my life years ago as a helpful secretary, and became my treasured companion and business manager and devoted helpmate. It was Jaime who compiled and published, just last year, *The End of the Road*, a collection of my songs and poems and columns published by George Palmer Putnam, a cousin of Jaime's. She did it as a surprise for me, and she has promised also to shepherd this new book into publication by G. P. Putnam Sons. We've agreed it is best she hold off publishing until a few years after my death and the death of a few others who might be hurt by my "True Confessions." Meanwhile, the manuscript remains in the collection of my work that Jaime has established at UCLA.

The decision to re-tell my life's story began with a wonderful charade, a joke of sorts. I cooked it up with my longtime friend Rose Moor Ives, a feature writer for the *Examiner*. I would never have then taken on the task of writing another book unless she agreed to be my editor. Rose has been that and much more, every step of the way.

Here's how it all began.

CHAPTER 2

MY OBITUARY

CARRIE JACOBS-BOND IS 82 YEARS OLD

> Los Angeles, Aug 28 (AP) White-haired Carrie Jacobs-Bond, the composer whose best known works were "The End of a Perfect Day" and "I Love You Truly," observed her eighty-second birthday today — and celebrated by reading her obituary to 500 persons assembled to honor her. "I wrote it in 1943," she told members of the breakfast club, "but it looks as if you folks won't get to read it, so I'll read it to you." It was a simple chronology of her life. Mrs. Bond said that she had been seriously ill for five months, but that "her health was now much improved."

Rose Ives filed this bland story with the Associated Press. The obituary was anything but "a simple chronology" of my life. It was lot more fun than that.

After arriving at a certain age, I found I was beginning my day by turning to the obituary page in the morning paper. Do you do that? My feelings are a mixture of sympathy for the departed and relief that my friends are not among them. I began to wonder how, when someone famous has passed away, the newspaper can print such a complete and well-researched article almost overnight. Rose explained it to me.

"Carrie, they're ready to go to print long before the person dies. The column's already written. All the editor does is fill in the blanks—the date, cause of death—it's easy."

"How do they decide on who deserves that?"

"The obit editor is constantly checking the file of clippings from past issues. Wouldn't you know—they call it the morgue. If a lot of copy has piled up about a person, somebody writes up their obituary in advance. You may be sure, dear Carrie, they are ready and waiting for you to die. You're practically in print."

I had a wicked idea. "Rose," I said, "Plans are already made for my annual birthday party at the Woman's Club on August 11th. Is there any way you could get me a copy of my own obituary from the *Examiner*? I fully intend to stay alive and disappoint them, but I think it would be fun if I read it at the party next month."

She howled. "You naughty girl! Yes, I'll sneak a carbon copy. You know it's bound to be very flattering, don't you?"

I said I supposed it would. "But Rose," I added, "I also know it will be full of mistakes and exaggerations. You newspaper people keep on repeating each other's stories and anecdotes until readers take them for gospel. I've lived in Hollywood long enough to know how it's done. Press agentry has become an art. Louella Parsons is a friend of mine, don't forget."

"Carrie Jacobs-Bond, you have never had a press agent in your life!"

"No I haven't, Rose. Never needed one. I've been my own press agent all these years."

"And the mistakes and exaggerations?"

"Decide for yourself," I said. "Get me that obituary soon as you can, and join us at the party."

We did it. The party, an annual affair, was a breakfast at the Los Angeles Woman's Club on Figueroa Street. 500 people were there: Kathleen Norris, dear Mary Pickford and Buddy, Henry Cadman, ailing but determined, Wallace Beery, Zazu Pitts, so many wonderful friends.

Good as her word, Rose had purloined, with time to spare, a copy of my latent obit from the *Examiner.*

When the moment came I rose and thanked everyone, especially my Master of Ceremonies, the director William Keighley. He had taken the occasion to announce Warner Brothers' plan for a picture about my life. I then proceeded to read from the *Examiner's* obituary, and at every sentence or so I corrected their "mistakes and exaggerations," and delivered my own versions. My friends had as much fun as I did. Frankly, I brought down the house. Hoping they would laugh, I kept in reserve an unusual quotation about me from the Oakland *Tribune* years ago. I'll get to that. Here's a copy of my talk—first, lines from the *Examiner's* obituary, then the responses of the birthday lady.

"Composer Carrie Jacobs-Bond died of a heart ailment at her Hollywood home on August 9th, two days before her 82nd birthday. She was best known for *A Perfect Day.*"

If I died on August 9th it would have been anything but a Perfect Day.

"The song achieved incredible popularity 30 years ago."

And 30 days ago. Nelson Eddy just recorded it again for Victor Records.

"The song has sold over 5,000,000 copies."

Incorrect. As of the end of my company's fiscal year on June 1st "A Perfect Day" had sold 6,459,800 copies. I should know, I own it and publish it. And count the money.

"Mrs. Bond was born in Janesville, Wisconsin, the daughter of a wealthy physician and his wife, a belle of New England society."

My father was a physician until he served two bloody years in a Civil War hospital. He gave up medicine when he came home and became a grain and commodity speculator. He lost everything when the Chicago wheat market crashed in 1870, and died when I was eight. My mother was from New England all right, but a "belle?" The only bells in her life were the wedding bells that clanged at each of her three marriages.

"Carrie Minetta Jacobs also chose to marry a physician, the distinguished Dr. Frank Lewis Bond."

It sounds like "shy young Wisconsin maid marries beloved country doctor," doesn't it? Ha! Frank Bond took me on my first real date when he was eighteen and I was fourteen. We went to a concert, the first I'd ever seen. Frank Bond was my first and only true love. I loved him truly.

"After the birth of their son Frederic in 1881, she and Dr. Bond moved to the state of Michigan, where he began a lucrative medical practice."

No. Frank Bond and I had a fight. I was eighteen by then, and out of spite I married another beau and had a baby. Seven years later I got a divorce and married Dr. Bond. (Am I beginning to sound like a movie star?) The "lucrative practice" in Michigan was way up north in the tough mining village of Iron River. This time the physician in the family speculated in mining stocks. We lost everything in the Panic of 1893.

"It was there that the happy girl-wife first composed little songs for her husband and lullabies for their son. Dr. Bond urged his wife to have these melodies published, believing they had too great merit to be known only in their own home."

I had been writing songs since I was four. Dr. Bond did urge me to write them down, but when I decided to try and sell a few of them down in Chicago—we needed money badly—he said what Grandfather had said to me years before—something like, 'I guess the men in this family will always be able to take care of the women folks.' We had quite a spat over that. I went to Chicago anyway and sold a pair of children's songs for thirty-five dollars cash. I did make some friends in Chicago who helped me hugely in the hard years ahead. Then I took myself to the Fair, rode the Ferris Wheel, and caught the train home.

"Later, crushed by the great sorrow of Dr. Bond's sudden death, she found her only solace in trying to realize the ambitions her husband had cherished for her."

They made that up. Just made it up! My ambitions, as always, were those of Carrie Jacobs.

"After seven difficult years in Chicago, during which Mrs. Bond ran a boarding house and painted china for a living, she finally sold two of her best-known songs, *Just A-Wearyin' for You* and *I Love You Truly.* They have made her a wealthy woman."

I never ran a boarding house, but winter after winter I took in hobos and desperate women and gave them a meal and a place to sleep in the dreary apartments I managed to find. I painted china, but make a living at it? Hardly. I found out first-hand about poverty and the people trapped within it, because I was one of them. I've been giving my money to the poor ever since. I did become a wealthy woman, thank you, but not by selling my songs. No Chicago publisher would take them. "Too arty," they said. So I started my own company on two-hundred-and-fifty borrowed dollars and published them myself. I've been in business ever since, and I stand before you this morning a tough old capitalist with an eye on the main chance.

"In addition to her songs, Mrs. Bond was the author of an autobiography and several stories for children."

The "several stories for children" so glibly dismissed include my Little Kitten Songs and Stories. *We published it, with sales of over half-a-million copies. I've been considering a re-write of the autobiography, also full of mistakes and exaggerations and quite a number of careful lies. It won't be published, however, until you've read my real obituary.*

I must say it was an altogether jolly breakfast. I thanked the audience for their friendship and especially their laughter. I felt I'd earned the right to close with a pat on the back from that Oakland critic of years ago.

> Were she not a composer first, Mrs. Bond would inevitably be an actress, and if she so chose, just as readily a comedienne.

I hope when the time comes somebody will put *that* in my obituary.

CHAPTER 3

THE THREE SONGS

"*Take Me Out to the Ball Game*, Mrs. Bond, by a long shot!" I had asked Albert Von Tilzer to name his most successful song. "Jack Norworth and I have made more money on that song," he said, "than all the rest of them put together. And neither of us had ever been to a ball game. We thought it was just another ditty."

Both he and Mr. Norworth moved to California a few years ago. (It seems like all the New York songwriters move out here to die.) And he was part of that wonderful ASCAP concert we all did in San Francisco a few years ago. Over lunch at the Brown Derby last year we got to comparing our songs. I told him I was bothered that after all my work, publishing over 200 of them, I seem to be remembered nowadays for only three: *The End of a Perfect Day, Just a-Wearyin' for You,* and *I Love You Truly.*

He laughed. "Mrs. Bond," he said, "count yourself lucky. They're like folk songs. Or even hymns. Everyone knows them. And don't tell me you're not making a fortune on them. Didn't I hear a new Ray

Noble record of *I Love You Truly* just last week? And what about John Kirby's jazz version? What more do you want?"

I asked him if it didn't bother him, too, that after all his years in music most of his songs were forgotten. "Not at all," he said. "I think a popular song is like a butterfly. A little time in the sun, and then it dies." He was quite serious. "Popular songs are all about fashion," he said. "Like moustaches, dance steps, skirt lengths. And movie stars. They're in style for a while and then they're gone. Jack and I wrote a lot better things than the baseball song, but baseball's never gone out of fashion. So aren't we lucky?"

"Do you think it's all luck?" I asked him.

"Don't you?" he said. "You just said *Shadows* was the best love song you ever wrote. Nobody's ever heard of it. Jack and I wrote *Honey Boy* back in o-seven—our best song ever, we think, and a big hit. Heard it lately?"

I remember the song, but had to admit I hadn't heard it for years. "Maybe you should try to get it in a movie," I said, half-serious. "I'll bet sales of *Put Your Arms Around Me, Honey* have spruced up since Betty Grable sang it in that picture." That pleased him. "You bet they have," he said, "and Lew Brown and I are keeping our fingers crossed since we heard Betty Hutton's singing *Oh, By Jingo!* in her new picture. Nothing like a good movie to bring back a song. Think of all those Cohan numbers Jim Cagney did in *Yankee Doodle Dandy*. Nobody'd heard them for years: *Mary, 45 Minutes from Broadway, Give My Regards to Broadway*. Now they're everywhere. Too bad George didn't live to enjoy it."

"Well, at least he was still alive," I said, "when *Over There* got popular again."

"You're right, Mrs. Bond. Remember what I said about popular songs and fashion? War is fashionable again these days."

I'm sure he didn't mean to hurt me with that. I think he'd forgotten that my biggest "hit" was a war song, too.

WHEN YOU COME TO THE END OF A PERFECT DAY
AND YOU SIT ALONE WITH YOUR THOUGHTS,
WHILE THE CHIMES RING OUT WITH A CAROL GAY
FOR THE JOY THAT THE DAY HAS BROUGHT,
DO YOU THINK WHAT THE END OF A PERFECT DAY

CAN MEAN TO A TIRED HEART,
WHEN THE SUN GOES DOWN WITH A FLAMING RAY
AND THE DEAR FRIENDS HAVE TO PART

Bond & Son published it in 1910, and we did a fair business with it for five or six years, until the war. Then—and I have no idea how or why—the doughboys in France adopted it. A reminder of home I suppose, and over here, a prayer for their safe return. We sold millions of copies.

I was born in 1862 during the bloodiest war in our history. As I sit down to work on this corrective to *The Roads of Melody*, another war is ending, the second one in my time designated "World." The Great War, as we called the 1917 version, brought me willy-nilly, not only world fame and wealth, but a saintly aura that seems to have come with it. *Perfect Day, w*ithout the war, might have languished on the shelves—out-of-fashion, as Mr. Von Tilzer would say. Instead, we've sold something over 6,000,000 copies to date, not to mention dozens of arrangements for barbershop quartets and concert bands and every other ensemble you can imagine.

I used to say how pleased I was that the boys went into battle singing my song and dreaming of home. How shameful of me. In spite of the money we made and still make from that song, it will always remind me of death in the trenches of France. And deeper down, every soldier's death returns me to stories of the blood-stained Civil War that haunted my family, a war that desolated my father's youth and, I'm quite sure, hastened his death.

And yet. And yet. My song was born in a rare moment of "peace and repose," as Mark Sullivan wrote in one of his wonderful *Our Times* books. I was on a motor trip with friends—a perfect day—and it came to me as we watched a gorgeous sunset near Riverside, California. We were stopping at the famous old Mission Inn, and I rushed back to my room with the words just pouring out of me—the poem, no music yet. Several months later, again on a drive with friends, this time crossing the Mohave Desert with moonlight now instead of sunset, the poem popped back into my head. Now finally it was laced with fragments of melody. I couldn't sleep that night until I finished it.

The song has long since taken on a life of its own—movies, plays, short stories, and cartoons. Last year MGM had me retell the Mission

Inn-Mohave story in one of those James A. Fitzpatrick "Travel Talk" short subjects. They called it "Along the Cactus Trail." Mr. Fitzpatrick and his crew met me at the Inn. It was still as enchanting as ever. They had me go over the story again. For the thousandth time. I wish I could say they made it interesting or fun, but Mr. Fitzpatrick's droning voice was as boring as ever, and they left out one of the best parts of the interview, I thought. I told one of the many jokes that went around when the song was first so popular. It's still my favorite and goes like this.

Carrie Jacobs-Bond was on her honeymoon. They were in Switzerland and had climbed to the top of a high peak at sunset. It was so breath-taking that in her wild enthusiasm she impulsively threw herself at her lover and he sailed over the cliff. He was killed instantly, and she rushed back to their hotel to write "This is the End of a Perfect Day."

Jokes aside, I've been asked a hundred times if there wasn't truly a romantic experience hiding in the story. Long ago I found the perfect answer: "Wouldn't you like to know?"

That droll fellow George Ade—another of the lasting friends I met on a magic night in Chicago years ago—wrote a play in 1915 under the title of my song. They made a picture out of it two years later—which I didn't go to see. I worried they were cashing in on the war craze. The sweetest time the song ever had in the movies was when that funny, lonesome-looking Sterling Holloway sang a whole chorus of it in *Remember the Night*, which I *did* see at the premiere at Graumann's Chinese a few years ago, sitting with the stars, Barbara Stanwyck and Fred MacMurray, and that dear Beulah Bondi, who I think stole the show. Preston Sturges wrote it, and he introduced me that night to the director, Mr. Liesen. They were sweet, and I joshed that their picture might become a classic as long as they kept my song in it. Mr. Liesen was very gallant, and said he hoped it would become halfway as classic as *Perfect Day.*

He congratulated me that Paul Robeson had just recorded it for Victor Records. I hadn't known, and I was thrilled. Robeson has such a big voice. Of course I'm pleased when anyone makes a record of one of my songs, even sweet old Henry Burr, who made one of the first cylinders with his thin little tenor. But I'm somehow thrilled all the more to hear big voices singing my little songs—Mr. Robeson, Alma Gluck, and Rosa Ponselle! My, she was wonderful. I'll bet you didn't know that she and her sister Carmela toured in vaudeville as "Those Tailored Italian

Girls." It was Caruso himself who heard Rosa and insisted she go right to the Metropolitan Opera when she was barely twenty. I never shared the bill with her in my brief vaudeville days on the Keith circuit, but we crossed paths often enough that she's found time to visit me occasionally at Grossmont—especially now that she's retired from the stage and managing her school for young singers back East. Rosa saw to it that I was sent copies of her Victor records, (she also sang *I Love You Truly*) but there've been so many other recordings all these years—still are—that I lose track. My Jaime Palmer doesn't, thank heavens. She keeps an eye on everything for me, especially the new records. "Let's see, Carrie," she said just the other day. "So far this year there's Morton Downey and Jeanette MacDonald and Andre Kostelanetz for Columbia. Oh, and Bing Crosby. Not bad for that old song!"

Now, forgive me, but Jaime and Rose have urged me to quote the critics now and again:

> She has a genius for writing songs that touch the heart. *Just A-Wearyin' for You, I Love You Truly* — these are familiar to hundreds of thousands, but almost the whole world knows *Perfect Day.*
>
> *American* Magazine

You see? The same Three Songs!

> JUST A-WEARYIN' FOR YOU
> ALL THE TIME A-FEELIN' BLUE,
> WISHIN' FOR YOU, WOND'RIN' WHEN
> YOU'LL BE COMIN' HOME AGAIN,
> RESTLESS, DON'T KNOW WHAT TO DO,
> JUST A WEARYIN' FOR YOU.

I had never heard of the Decca record company. It seemed for years that everything was from either Victor or Columbia. And then in 1934 there was quite a hubbub when Bing Crosby—he was already such a big star—made his first record for this new company. My songs were on both sides! *Just a'Wearyin' for You* and *I Love You Truly*. We didn't even know about it for quite a while. You see, they don't have to tell you or ask permission, just as long as they get a license and pay the

royalty. Which they did and they have done ever since. M
checks have rolled in!

I hope you understand that as the composer *and* the publisher, Bond & Son receives the entire sum! It's still just two cents for each record. I suppose that doesn't sound like much, but when a record sells thousands of copies, it adds up. I liked the way he sang. Of course he's now a big star in pictures, too, especially since he's teamed up with Bob Hope in those silly "road" pictures. My friend Donald Meek was in one of Bing's movies—*Pennies from Heaven*—back in 1936, and escorted me to the opening. We met the composer, Arthur Johnston, and I told him how I loved his new song. I also met Mr. Crosby. He seemed rather distant and cold, but that hasn't kept the checks from rolling in.

Just a Wearyin' for You was published in our first folio. I called it *Seven Songs as Unpretentious as a Wild Rose.* That's when I first painted roses on my covers. I'd been painting on china ever since I could remember, and in those dreary Chicago days it helped to pay the rent. People have asked me ever since why I called it "Unpretentious." It was partly because I was so put off by the garish sheet music coming from Tin Pan Alley in those days—awful, artless covers that just seemed to shout "Buy Me!" I wanted something simple. Frederic teased that, in a way, it was pretentious of me to call my songs "unpretentious." I don't think he ever understood how unsure of myself I was then. Remember, the Chicago publishers had refused to take the songs in any form. And every one of them advised me that people would never buy a book of songs, only single sheets. And I decided not to bother with the fractions of a dollar. "That won't do, Mrs. Bond," one of them said. "At least mark them 98 cents." But *Seven Songs*, I decided, would sell for a dollar even. That way we wouldn't have to bother with small change. Remember, for the first several years, we sold our music directly to the Chicago music stores. Frederic took it around on his bicycle, then later when we could afford it, on his motorcycle. In the little hall bedroom of our tiny Chicago rooming house he installed some shelves. The depth of the closet was just the width of the music. That was our very first stock room, the seed of all my future business.

Just a-Wearyin' for You taught me my first lesson in how the music business really works. You see, I had very little belief in my own verses. At first I wrote them myself because I had no one as a partner, and no money to pay someone. I saw a poem "Just a-Wearyin' for You" in a Chicago newspaper. I'm ashamed to admit I had no idea of copyrights. I thought that when a poem was printed without the author's name, especially in a newspaper, anyone could use it. We had just printed my song, using all the words, when I found the poem was written by Frank L. Stanton, and had been published several years before by the D. Appleton Company in New York.

I was worried sick. Who in the world could advise me of what to do? I thought of John McCutcheon, another of those talented fellows I had met with Amber Holden at the Bohemian Club in Chicago a few years before. His sister Jessie and I had become friends, and she said go to John and tell your story. I thought he'd scold me for my ignorance, but instead he said, "I think you should go right to New York and see Mr. Appleton himself. I know him, and I'll give you a letter. I'm sure when he hears your story he'll believe you."

I felt like a criminal. I had nightmares about a lawsuit—the awful things that can happen to people who plagiarize other people's ideas. I spent nearly every penny I had on a ticket to New York, sitting up all night in a chair coach with my lunch in a paper bag. But thanks to John's letter, I met with Mr. Appleton immediately, and he did believe my story—and my innocence. "It's true, Mrs. Bond," he said, "we do own the poem. We bought all the rights. But you're welcome to use it for your song." I waited until I left his office before weeping with joy and relief. "We'll draw up a simple contract," he said. "Come in tomorrow."

They had published the poem in a little book called "Songs of the Soil." Mr. Stanton received royalties from the sale of the book and from then on, from my song. D. Appleton would administer them both. All we had to do in our next printing was add, in very small type,"Words by Permission, D. Appleton & Co."

I made it my job to learn more about Frank Stanton, that he'd worked in Atlanta all his life at the newspaper there, and had written so much poetry he was named Georgia's Poet Laureate. I was so intimidated by his reputation I didn't have the nerve to get in touch with him until years later. When I did, he wrote back the sweetest letter, thanking me for all the royalty checks he'd gotten from Bond & Son by way of D. Appleton—a hundred times, he said, what he'd earned from his little book of poems.

I found I'd done another stupid "plagiarism" thing with a verse called "Poor Little Lamb," by a man named Paul Lawrence Dunbar. He had written me that I had used his verse without permission, and would I come to see him. After my happy meeting with Mr. Appleton, I went to see Mr. Dunbar the next day. I hadn't thought until then that he was a negro—a very quiet, dignified man with the most wonderful speaking voice I have ever heard. We talked of our troubles, and I realized mine were nothing compared to his—a colored genius who longed for recognition as a poet, in a country just forty years from slavery. He asked me to sing the little lamb song for him. He seemed pleased, even rather moved. He gave me the permission, and then went on to ask if I would use several other of his poems for my songs. One of them I'm sure expressed his personal yearning: *The Last Long Rest.* He died not long after, but I hope you know that he's now widely praised. His fame, sadly, came far too late. Bond & Son published three more songs "by Carrie Jacobs-Bond and Paul Lawrence Dunbar." I'm very proud to have "collaborated" with him.

This New York visit provided me a first-class education in how the music business worked. My weighty problems had been solved, this time, by the fair-minded Mr. Appleton and Mr. Dunbar. I mightn't be so fortunate in the future. I left the city resolving that from then on, Carrie Jacobs-Bond would own the music *and* the words of all her songs.

> What is there about *Just A-Wearyin' for You* that clutches the heart? Why has the simple ballad of *The End of a Perfect Day* become the greatest heartsong ever written? What is the charm of *I Love You Truly* that makes it a fitting tribute when a man and a woman are joined in matrimony?
>
> Los Angeles *Examiner*

I LOVE YOU TRULY, TRULY DEAR,
LIFE WITH ITS SORROW, LIFE WITH ITS TEAR,
FADES INTO DREAMS WHEN I FEEL YOU ARE NEAR,
FOR I LOVE YOU TRULY, TRULY DEAR.

Frank Bond died in December of 1895. It took a few weeks to settle my affairs in Iron River. Then I went back, heart-broken, to Janesville. I had no idea what I should do. Frederic would soon to be fifteen, and his schooling was interrupted again. (As it turned out, interrupted for good. He never went back.) For a few months I thought to somehow take up my life in Janesville again, after my seven years in Iron River. I had a bit of money left from Dr. Bond's insurance.

My piano came down with us to the cottage I'd rented for Frederic and me, and in those dark winter months of 1896 I composed three songs. Two of them would join *Perfect Day* to become "My Three Songs," and mark my life ever after. I dedicated all three to Frank's memory, and five years later, when we published my *Seven Songs* folio in Chicago, his initials remained over the title of *Just a-Wearyin' for You*. As you know, I didn't write the words, but Frank Stanton's poem, the title alone, spoke to my grief, and I embraced it. At the time, though, I was sure that another of the three, *Shadows*, would stand as my true farewell to Frank Bond. It spoke directly to my loss: "...the days are all too long, dear, the nights are longer still..."

Shadows never became the least bit popular. To be honest, I realize I'd committed the songwriter's cardinal sin: I wrote for myself, not the public. I've never forgotten that lesson. People want words of hope—of life going on in spite of it all—not reminders of death. And they don't want to hear *your* troubles.

I must have seen into the future when I wrote my third Janesville song. The words of *I Love You Truly* are in the present, not the past tense: "Life with its sorrow, life with its tear, fades into dreams when I feel you are near, for I love you truly, truly dear." I wrote those words thinking of Frank, yes. But he was gone. Somehow I must have sensed beneath my pain that love does come again, in different ways, at unexpected times. When this song for Frank Bond was finally published in 1901, it was dedicated to "A.B.H." In Chapter 15, I reveal a name to go with those initials.

I Love You Truly wasn't officially copyrighted until 1906. We somehow failed to file it with the others in the *Seven Songs* folio. No one spotted the error until we decided to publish it in a single sheet in 1906. Believe me, Frederic mailed that copyright application Special Delivery the next morning. That mistake could have been a disaster, but it turned out to have been a money-maker. Copyrights, you may know, are granted in two terms of 28 years each, 56 years if renewed. Since *I Love You Truly* wasn't under copyright until 1906, it will still be good until 1962 (1906 plus 56), earning full royalties on sheet music and records.

No, Dear Reader, I don't expect to be on earth in 1962. I'd be 100 years old! But the estate of Bond & Son will keep growing. (*Perfect Day* is good until 1966.) I think you'll be surprised and pleased when we announce publicly where the money will go. I intend to "spill the beans" on my 85th birthday.

Of "My Three Songs," *I Love You Truly* has earned by far the most in royalties from recordings — or "mechanicals" as they're called. It has become a favorite waltz! I composed it in 2/4 time and that's how we have always published it. But they tell me that Wayne King, the "Waltz King," plays it at every dance, and has recorded it three times. It turns out the melody fits just fine in three-quarter time, and who am I to complain? Our royalties are the same in 3/4 as in 2/4! On top of that, *I Love You Truly* has become a standard piece at weddings, along with *Because* and *Oh Promise Me,* and those Wagner and Mendelssohn wedding marches. I would never have dreamed of that!

Once in a while a song finds a life of its own. *Perfect Day* became a war song, and *I Love You Truly* a wedding anthem. It's been used over and over in the movies, tied almost every time to a wedding. We've lost count of the pictures that have used it, but we think the first one — just a year or two after sound came in — was a film about Jenny Lind, called *A Lady's Morals.* Grace Moore played the role, and again a song of mine found its way to an unforgettable voice. I have no idea why my little songs have come to be honored by such voices! The range of *I Love You Truly* is less than an octave. It couldn't be more simple. I composed it for small, private voices, I suppose, like my own. Yet here, at the end of my life, I can glory in all those wondrous singers — David Bispham and Jesse Bartlett Davis from the old days in Chicago; early records by Schumann-Heinck and Alma Gluck and new ones every year it seems, from stars like Jan Peerce and Lauritz Melchior. And now the movies! Grace Moore, and just a few years back, Lily Pons in a wonderfully funny picture with Jack Oakie and a saucy redhead named Lucille Ball.

I wish Frederic could have lived to see and hear our music in all these pictures! He would have been thrilled. They've used hardly any song but *I Love You Truly*, but that wouldn't have kept him from smiling as he endorsed the checks from RKO, United Artists, Sam Goldwyn — and Warner Brothers. Three or four years ago Warners did *The Bride Came C.O.D.* Jimmy Cagney and Bette Davis are in it. It may be my favorite because it was directed by William Keighley. Jaime and I attended the opening and met Mr. Keighley, and before I knew it, he was talking about making a picture about my life. He's been away with the armed forces, but I hear from him now and again. Now that the war is over he seems determined to go to work on it. He wants to cast Grace Moore as Carrie Jacobs-Bond! That beautiful woman? With that beautiful voice? He laughed when I said he'd be smarter to star Edna May Oliver. The laugh was on me. She died a year later.

I Love You Truly was in *We're Rich Again* — 1935, I think. Such a delightful picture with Edna May Oliver and Billie Burke, both of whom I adore — so funny. I met Edna May in my Chicago days. She was touring with an orchestra as their pianist. My, what a talented woman. She knew she was plain, but she took what she called "her horse face" and made a career of it. Everyone thought she was British because she played in so many films based on the stories of Charles Dickens, but she was from back East somewhere. I went with Beulah Bondi and a group of friends to her funeral at Forest Lawn. It was three years ago — just two weeks after my beloved May Robson died.

Beulah and I often chat about that other picture — the one with Sterling Holloway singing *Perfect Day*. And bless her heart, she is going to arrange for me to see the preview of a new one she's making with Jimmy Stewart. She plays his mother, like she did in *Mr. Smith Goes to Washington*. It's another one of Mr. Frank Capra's movies, and she says it's very different — quite sad really, but with a happy ending. It's called *The Greatest Gift*, but Beulah says they're going to change the title. They're shooting it at a studio I'd never heard of called Liberty Pictures. She telephoned to let me know they had just shot a scene where two actors — one of them is Ward Bond — serenade the just-married Mr. Stewart and his bride with an entire chorus of *I Love You Truly*. Lionel Barrymore is in the cast, that wonderful Thomas Mitchell, and a lot of children. It'll be released next year, Beulah says, and I can't wait to see it. I think Mr. Stewart is just about my favorite actor these days. And yes, I'll be pleased with checks from Liberty Pictures.

I treasure my Hollywood friends, and can no longer imagine my life as it would have been, had I stayed in Chicago or Janesville — or if Frank Bond had lived, spending my life in Iron River. Not that I've ever wanted an active part in the motion picture business here — it seems just too frantic and precarious. I've been approached a few times to play small roles as a music teacher or a "fading star," but I don't think at my age, with my aches and pains, I'd be up to the rigors of movie-making. Those glamorous people — the ones that stay in the business for very long — are tough people, with endless patience. Making a movie is nothing but hard work. When May (Robson) finished a picture, she couldn't wait to spend a few weeks with me in the quiet of Grossmont.

My one little movie venture, other than the James Fitzpatrick travelogue, was a pleasant-enough little short subject I made in 1933. Edwin C. Hill — that fellow with the familiar radio voice who does the "human side of the news," — narrated a look-in on a day in the life of Carrie Jacobs-Bond at the Pinehurst house. I didn't sing or even speak, but they followed me around, playing with the pups and showing the garden. They added some whiny organ music under Mr. Hill's voice, but the songs were good. Three of my songs are on the soundtrack — yes, those Three Songs — sung by a young fellow they call "The Dream Singer," Ralph Kirbery. His is a lovely voice, a bit like Bing Crosby's or Dick Powell's — but deeper. I didn't meet Mr. Kirbery until after they had put the film together, at a party at the home of the director, a Mr. McGuire. I haven't heard or seen anything of him since.

Jaime Palmer insisted I close this chapter with some hard figures. She has said to me time and again, "Carrie, your life won't be the least bit interesting to people today unless you say how much money you've made." I said it was not the time to talk about my estate — that would have to wait till they read my will. "Fine," she said, "Just give the number of sheet music sales — and only for the three big hits if you want. They can do the rest — at fifty cents a copy."

I'm sure you know that when you pay fifty cents for a copy for one of my songs at a music store, Bond & Son gets only a little bit of that. The retailer, the wholesaler, the distributor — they each get their mark-up. And then there are the costs of production: the art work, engraving, printing, shipping. Frederic used to estimate that Bond & Son got between six and eight cents per copy when all was said and done. Bear that in mind when I tell you that up to the end of last year — and these are round numbers, *Perfect Day* sold 6,500,000, *I Love You Truly* 8,200,000, and *Just a-Wearyin' for You* 2,400,000. I won't ignore sales of my other songs either, many still in print. *Lonely Hour, The Hand of You, Little Lost Youth of Me* — those are some of my favorites and there were almost two hundred others. You may be as surprised as I was. When Jaime added up sales for other than the Three Songs, the total for all them put together came to just a little over 300,000 copies. The grand total? Around 18,000,000.

And remember, these numbers are just for single sheets. I have no idea how much we've sold in quartet and choral versions, band and orchestra arrangements, transcriptions for mandolin and banjo ensembles, brass quintets and whatnot. There again, though, 99% were of the Three Songs.

I appeared once on Sigmund Spaeth's NBC radio program "The Tune Detective." He's quite an imposing scholar and an equally imposing man, six-foot-six at least, with a very big voice and even bigger ego. I do like his books on the history of popular music, and he has said some nice things about me, even though he couldn't resist criticizing *Just a-Wearyin' for You.* He wrote that it was "...an immediate success in spite of the atrocious accent in the title phrase." He meant the accent in "Just a-weary-IN' for you." I was able to tease him about it. I told him before the broadcast that it hadn't affected our income from the song one bit. He got back at me in a rather sarcastic way. I had brought along sheet music for the Three Songs, and I saw him scanning them quickly. When we went on the air, the first thing he said was, "My guest today is Carrie Jacobs-Bond. She has written three lasting popular hits: *Just a-Wearyin' for You, I Love You Truly* and *The End of a Perfect Day.* I have just checked them carefully, and can report to you that milady's well-deserved fame and fortune is based on a total of just forty-six measures of music." I had never thought of it like that, but in a way he was right.

I reached over and removed the Great Man's fountain pen from his vest pocket. His notebook was lying open on the table near the microphone, and while he rattled on about how the melody of *Perfect Day* is obviously based on Raff's *Cavatina* and possibly something from *Faust*, I scribbled some simple arithmetic. He stopped long enough to ask me what I was doing, and I said, "You're right, Mr. Spaeth. About those forty-six measures. And you know something? As of today that works out to about $31,000 per measure. How's your new book selling?"

CHAPTER 4

EMMA AND HANNIBAL

An Ojibwa woman named Auntie Mamma pulled me out of my mother one afternoon in August of 1862 and cut the cord with her teeth. Mother didn't tell me that little detail until after I was married to Ed Smith and pregnant with Frederic in the spring of 1881. Auntie Mamma was still alive and Mother planned for her to midwife me, but she died a month before my boy was born.

Janesville's revered midwife had an unpronounceable Indian name, and "Auntie Mamma," was as close as the townspeople could come to it. The settlers were an impatient lot. Those long Indian words and names had to be twisted into something that sounded like English. I didn't know until I was in sixth grade that we called our Ojibwa tribes "Chippewa" because when an Indian said "Ojibwa," it sounded something like "Chippewa" to white people. I came to be grateful for my childhood exposure to the peaceful tribes around Janesville. It prepared me for the much closer and often dangerous contact with the Lake Superior Ojibwas when I moved up north to Iron River with Frank Bond.

Auntie Mamma had lived almost a hundred years — no one knew for sure. But people loved to marvel that she was born in the days when the colonies back East were becoming the United States of America. There was never a time when I was a child that I wasn't aware of her. She not only delivered babies, she delivered the mail in Janesville and Johnstown Center for years. Wherever she went two or three of her dogs went along. She had a dozen of them. My grandfather told me she ate one every so often, but Mother said that was nonsense. Auntie Mamma was an outsized, husky woman with a deeply-wrinkled face, no teeth you could see, but eyes and ears sharp as a cat. Years later I put her in one of my "Old Man" poems that were so popular. She spoke a little English only when she had to, but her command of French was part of her mystery, with whispers and rumors of a long-ago love for a trapper from Quebec. Village gossips reported that every spring three strapping Frenchmen from Canada visited their grandmother (or great-grandmother) bringing gifts and money.

Her life in Rock County had begun long before the white race carved Wisconsin into towns and counties and named them after presidents and pioneers. Our county was named after the Rock River, logically enough. It was and is a rocky place, and at one time was, I suppose, quite breathtaking. Janesville was named for the itinerant Mr. Janes, who made the first claims along the river and then went on west. The town finally got going when a man named St. John came over from Milwaukee and built a mill on the river, where the rock narrowed and the river could be forded. So of course he called it Ford Mill. As a little girl I was confused, then delighted when I learned that my mother's sister, dear Aunt Abbie (Davis), had married a man named Jonas Ford, who bought the mill shortly after the war. How very clever, I thought. He didn't have to change its name!

My mother was Abbie's sister Imogene, or "Emma." She was a voluptuous woman. No one would have used that word in her day. They might have said "full-bodied," possibly "earthy." I knew she was also a beautiful woman. There were other beautiful women in Janesville, but I thought they were cold in their beauty, even frightened by it. Men sought them out, of course. But I've come to understand that men, seeking women, are driven as much by competition as by desire. With my mother it was somehow different. I watched how men hovered about her. I think they saw, not haughtiness in her beauty, but an unspoken understanding of their hungers.

I don't imply she was wayward. She married at seventeen, and I'm quite sure Hannibal Jacobs was her first love, and that she was faithful to him and he to her. Growing up as their only child, I would watch them, see the looks, the touches, the little links of private language that passed between them. I know I was jealous of Mother, convinced I was a plain child and would never be beautiful like her. My father loved me too — I knew that. But I first became aware of the selfishness in my nature when I realized I wanted to come between my parents, and couldn't.

I still have a faded daguerreotype of my father when he was twenty or so. I thought him quite handsome, in the stiff way of those early portraits. The man I remember from my childhood was already overweight and losing his hair, but vigorous and full of fun. His eyes were the deepest brown I've ever seen, and he prided himself on his sharp vision. He was a constant reader, a pretty fair flutist, and the man to beat, they said, in a game of horseshoes.

Father had trained as a physician in New York before he came west to marry Imogene Davis. How he and Emma managed their courtship I have no idea, what with half a continent between them. But manage they did, and were married in Janesville in 1859. When I was born three years later Father was not there to celebrate. He was on active duty in the Union Army as a company surgeon in the 7th Wisconsin Infantry alongside the illustrious Dr. William Palmer. I think the horrors of those years of service to the wounded and dying at the York Union hospital drove Father from medical practice. When he came home he went into the grain and commodities business — he and Grandfather Davis — speculating, actually, until the grain market crashed in 1870 and they lost everything. Grandfather somehow managed to keep the hotel, where I was fated to spend much of my childhood. Father was bankrupt.

The two happiest periods in my long life were both of seven years. The first was my childhood in the lovely brick house on Pleasant Street in Janesville. It ended on February 21st, 1870. Father died, suddenly and in terrible pain. His death was always described by whispering neighbors with a word that haunts me still — *mysterious* . The second seven were the sweet and loving years I spent as the wife of Dr. Frank

Bond. Those sevens may have been happy, but they were not lucky. Frank Bond died at thirty-seven in a death not mysterious but absurd.

As a child, I wondered why my parents had no other children. I begged them for a little brother or sister. We were surrounded by large families. Most were hard-working farm families, the more hands the better. Even Mother's town friends had children by the half-dozen. After all, most babies just *happened.* The only sure way to avoid them was total abstinence. I had heard the grownups say that my birth had somehow damaged Mother's ability to have another baby, but it wasn't so. I learned from her years later that they had didn't have another child because they *didn't want one*! They were determined to protect the secret world of their love for each other. It was strong. A child hears sounds at night and sees smiles and nudges next morning. Believing they wanted no more children made me question, as a little girl, if they had wanted me. Not, by the way, that they ever withheld their affection. I was a loved and loving child.

A year after Father's death Emma Jacobs married John Phelps Williams.

I was devastated. I disliked Williams and could not bear the idea of his taking the place of my father. I was too young to understand the depth of my mother's grief and loneliness. And far too young to admire her determination to go on with life, meet her own needs, return to financial security after Father's bankruptcy. Williams was the first man in Janesville to go into the new-fangled business of insurance. He had been a frequent dinner guest in our home, and I childishly convinced myself he had cheated Father somehow in the grain debacle. I knew he was "sweet on" my mother, but then so was every man in Janesville. I refused to imagine she gave to this man the kind of love she had shared with my father.

So began the years I lived at the Davis House with grandfather and his wife. Mr. Williams and his new bride had moved over to the nearby town of Milton. I saw Mother often enough, but it was a lonely time. My health was poor and I longed for her touch and her words of encouragement. I retreated into music and painting and poetry. Living at the hotel I missed out on the close friendships girls make at that age. I'm sure the emptiness of those days accounts for the profound value I have placed on friendship ever since. You will see, as the years go by, that my music and my friends will literally become my life.

I missed my mother terribly, but as I got older I realized she was teaching me two lessons. The first warned me how deep the love between man and woman can be and how devastating is its loss. The second taught me to look out for myself, even though in so doing I might hurt others, even those I love. I had no idea how soon I would apply both lessons to my own life.

Mother and John Williams were married for seven years or so, until he died while on a business trip somewhere in Iowa. They had no children. Mother's needs brought her in a matter of months into a third marriage in June of 1880. I was seventeen, and my own first marriage would take place Christmas Day of that year. Mother's new husband was Jim Minor, a family friend and a one-time suitor of Aunt Abbie Ford. Minor had worked at Ford's Mill as a young man and had then gone into the shoe trade, opening a retail shop in downtown Janesville. A year later I was stunned — as I'm sure were the matrons of Janesville — when my forty-one-year-old Mother gave birth to a baby boy. She and her husband James Minor swore they wanted the child, but I doubt it. I seldom saw my half-brother. Those who did will tell you that little Jimmy Minor went through life with a look of surprise on his face.

Mother and Jim Minor seemed happy. He was prospering, she was active and beautiful as ever. Janesville thought it the perfect marriage, and it lasted for sixteen years until Imogene Davis Jacobs Williams Minor filed for divorce in 1895. In December of that year she had rushed up to Iron River and was with me at Frank Bond's bedside as he died in agony. She said nothing about trouble at home. A divorce was granted in June of '96. Friends said Jim Minor was inconsolable. Six months later he took his own life.

At that point, my indomitable mother gave up on marriage but not, I'm sure, on love. There were men, but she had a life to live and a child to raise. Inspired I suppose by her years with the physician Hannibal Jacobs, she turned to a career in medicine herself and went into nursing. I saw almost nothing of her during those many years, and I still harbor some bitterness that she didn't offer help to Frederic and me when we were literally fighting for our lives in the desperate Chicago years of the late '90s.

When she retired in 1912 she was financially independent, but at my urging followed us later here to California. She bought a lovely bungalow in Altadena, and spent her last years gardening and earning master points at bridge. She was ninety-two when she died in 1932, strong and selfish as ever. I wish I could have inherited her stamina, but I think I have used her lessons in self-will to better ends than she. Obviously, I share her endowment of longevity. At eighty-three I am the mistress of a beautiful garden, and am considering taking up the game of bridge.

CHAPTER 5

MY SILVER SPOON

It may seem frivolous to recount a silly little incident that took place in Janesville when I was a child. But it has stuck with me ever since, so it must speak to me yet about having money, losing it, and having it again.

One day when I was about five, I overheard one of those remarks an adult considers offhand but a child never forgets. It wasn't said in a mean way, really, but I knew it had a jealous edge to it. We were in the lobby of Davis House. There was always some kind of Sunday get-together at the hotel — a church social, maybe a wedding reception or just as likely, a wake. There I was, clinging to my father's hand, crushed in the tangle of the grownup's long Sunday skirts and blue serge trousers, trapped down there near their smelly boots and dripping galoshes. I was desperate to be home at the piano so I could work out one of the hymns we'd sung at Morning Prayer. It was still ringing in my head, and I knew I'd have to hurry to find it on the keys before it went away.

Grandfather should just have called that place the Davis Hotel. "Davis House" sounds grand and elegant, which it wasn't. It was a three-storey frame building of twenty or so rooms, with rickety stairs and no fire escapes. If you were lodged on the third floor and fire broke out, you were supposed to descend on a heavy rope, bolted to the window frame in each room. Big knots were tied every three or four feet in the rope for you to grip as you clambered down. I'm telling you this because the Davis House did burn down in 1883, but no one died, so I guess the ropes were strong and the roomers courageous.

The Davis House was "modern," meaning there were two communal toilets or "water closets." For years I was far too shy to use one of them. Grandfather was ever so proud of them. He bragged all over town when he had them installed. Huge oaken water tanks mounted on cast iron pipes sent water rushing down into the white porcelain bowls below. You pulled the heavy brass chain and gravity did the rest. Children were instructed not to watch this gurgling disappearance of our efforts, but the novelty was irresistible. After all, until the flush toilets came along, females — and males too, in frigid weather — had to employ the chamber pot provided in each room. (Father called them thunder mugs.) The hotel also had a set of outhouses, but only men and boys went out there.

And homes, of course, were still cursed with the outhouse. My mother insisted on calling ours the "back house." Father always said "privy." In any outhouse it was always either too hot or too cold, ours included, although it seemed nicer than most. There was a big iron hook for the coal-oil lantern if you had to go in there at night, which I never did until I was fifteen or so. Someone had tacked cartoons of General Grant on the inside of the door, and there were old copies of *Leslie's* magazine and the Janesville *Gazette* in a rack above the wooden slab you sat on. Ours had two openings, side by side — what the men called a two-holer. I couldn't imagine ever sitting in there with anyone else, even one of my parents. I was shocked and even a little jealous when I'd see them go in together, laughing and chatting.

The boys in the neighborhood pushed over as many outhouses as they could on Halloween. Ours was too big and heavy, so instead they chalked nasty words on the door. And we girls forever had to endure a chorus of catcalls and whistles from the neighborhood gang whenever they spotted us creeping in. Their embarrassed fathers dished out many

a thrashing, I'm sure, but that didn't change the boys' habits for long. Frequent encounters with dad's razor strap were routine, it seemed — just a part of growing up. Meanwhile, how in the world we managed our bodily needs in those Victorian times I have no idea. Children understood they were never to speak of such matters. I don't know about the boys, but as for the girls, our parents spooned in the castor oil and milk of magnesia and hoped for the best.

The lobby of Davis House was jammed with overstuffed horsehair sofas and chairs. There was a low table near the front window, smothered in newspapers. Ugly landscape paintings in gold frames covered every wall. Three spittoons were provided for the trade, plus another behind the reception desk. The spit for that one was produced mainly by Mr. Duggan, a part time clerk who had come back from Antietam with just one leg. One day he showed me his wooden one and let me write my name on it. I could smell his breath and knew right away it was from whisky, like Grandfather's. Mr. Duggan had been a lumberjack before the war, and still had big arms and shoulders that helped him get around pretty well on his crutch and good leg. I could tell he'd been a handsome boy when he went off to fight. Mother said he'd been one of Janesville's leading lady-killers. But by the time he worked for Grandfather he was fat and gruff. And lonely, I guess. Mr. Duggan moved over to Milwaukee after a few years, where Mother said he drank up his pension and died.

My favorite person at the hotel desk was Minnie Malzac. She had been Grandpa Davis's sister-in-law. His first wife, Nancy Malzac Davis, died when I was seven. Grandfather let just enough time go by to seem right and proper and married Minnie. That made me very happy, because right away I had a new Grandma I liked far better than the old one. It was said the Malzac family hailed from Budapest. I later came to realize that Nancy and Minnie were Gypsies. Nancy spent her short life denying it, Minnie reveling in it. She smelled of exotic places and wore clothing like no other woman in Janesville — big billowy skirts and shawls of every color sewn together. She decorated herself with what to a little girl seemed acres of necklaces and rings and pearl combs in her long auburn hair. When she was on duty behind the desk a bowl of peppermints or horehound drops was sure to appear. Minnie held me when I was upset and sang to me in a language I never heard anywhere else. Most of Janesville's citizens thought she was sort

of crazy, and maybe she was, a little bit. But to me she was a window to another world, and I loved her dearly. She would coax me into singing my little songs for her, and after I began playing the piano she would come over and sit by me sometimes and play a few bass notes, and sing and sigh in that other language.

She lived a long life, and I think she gave Grandpa a kind of love Grandma Nancy had not. I noticed that soon after he married Minnie, he didn't smell of whisky hardly at all, just wine every once in a while.

Mr. Duggan was on duty the day I heard that hurtful remark. I was hiding in a little cubby hole near the reception desk where I could watch him take off his wooden leg, when I overheard some woman say, "That lucky little Carrie Jacobs! *She was born with a silver spoon in her mouth."* Harmless enough, really, but I was bewildered. I remember running my little finger around my teeth trying to find the spoon and deciding I must have swallowed it. Those silly words have stayed with me all these years, perhaps because a lot of the things that have happened to me since haven't had much silver about them.

But the lady was right about my having "silver" at the time — at least for my first seven years. I was a happy child, cosseted by loving parents and grandparents and some aunts and uncles — memories of whom are now fuzzy but warm and comforting even so. In the town of Janesville, Wisconsin, during the years right after the war, Hannibal Jacobs could very well have adorned his only child's mouth with a spoon of silver. Father was on the way to becoming the richest man in the county. He had returned from Civil War service in 1864 and had abandoned any further practice of medicine. Postwar prosperity was in the air, much like we're counting on again today with *this* war over at last. He and Grandfather Davis opened an office near the hotel at Main and Milwaukee, and began their six-year spree in the dangerous game of speculation. Years later, Minnie, by then Grandfather's widow told me, "Those two! They were like a pair of riverboat gamblers." They speculated in everything, she recalled — beans, wheat and corn, pork, other commodities, and then in land claims. "Why, Carrie," she said, "they even tried to start a new town over there west of the river — called it 'Rockport,' — sold empty lots, mostly to New England people." They made good money according to Minnie, before the business bottomed out in the grain scandals of 1870.

So for a few years the Jacobs family was considered a member of Janesville's Upper Crust, what there was of it. Our house on Pleasant Avenue was pretentiously labeled "Italianate" by the Janesville *Gazette.* It was special for its time I suppose — not a frame house like all the others, but a handsome two-storey square brick with a cupola on top. I used to tell people I was born up there. Mother always scolded me for that, but I wonder. When I hear parents reprimanding their children for telling what they see as fibs, I wonder if it's wise. Sometimes the harmless fib of a child simply reveals a healthy imagination. I truly believed I was born up in that cupola. To me it was the nicest part of the house. And very secret.

From our huge front porch we could look out over fifteen acres planted in flowers and vegetable gardens, apple trees, and a grape arbor. I had my own bedroom as soon as I was liberated from the tiny nursery off my parent's big room. The piano sat in a front room called the Parlor in those days. It was my favorite room, on the south side of the house, looking out on the porch. The sun poured in most days of the year and brightened a room meant to be dark and severe. The wallpaper was patterned in ferns and flowers that my imagination turned constantly into the faces of saints and monsters. There was a heavy glass-covered bookcase bulging with dull brown medical books, a set of Shakespeare, and a few books by Hawthorne and Cooper and Washington Irving. Our Parlor had its own monkey stove, so the good smell of wood smoke blended with floor wax and wet dog — my dear pup Schneider, about whom I'll soon tell you.

Mr. and Mrs. Jacobs didn't restrict the Parlor to Sunday visits and special occasions like most families did. It was open to my friends and me for games and fun day or night. And when I was alone, I could sit in there for hours with my best friend of all, that quiet piano, searching for ways to bring it to life.

CHAPTER 6

THE ROSEWOOD

They say that even before my fourth birthday I could pick out airs on the piano with one finger. My father and mother were soon taking turns at singing or whistling tunes for me to play. That first piano — it had been grandfather's wedding gift to my mother — was the loveliest piano I have ever seen. Yes, *ever* seen — I can say that even today. It was what they called a "square grand" — not an upright or a real grand piano, but a sort of in-between. The cabinet was of carved rosewood and the keys of ebony and mother-of-pearl, not ivory. The backboard was inlaid with lovely flowers and birds of paradise also in mother-of-pearl. The music desk was intricately carved with scrolls just large enough that I could load them with empty wooden spools, pretending they were organ stops and I was a famous organist.

On this piano I discovered at first the tunes of others. But these were soon joined by dozens of my own. From the time I was that little girl, I thought of myself as a songwriter. Just sitting there I heard beautiful music that seemed to flow directly from my mind into my fingers. In quiet moments yet today, I hear exquisite melodies just as lovely, but they have never moved as easily to the keys of a piano, even to those of my beautiful Steinway, as they did on that dear old Rosewood.

Mother sold it soon after Father's death. She had married Mr. Williams, and said they needed the money in their move over to the town of Milton. That was three heartbreaks in a row: Father died, Mother re-married, and (worst of all?), I lost the Rosewood. That's when I went to live at the hotel. Minnie ordered Grandfather over to Chicago to buy another piano for me, and he came back to Janesville on the train with a second-hand Janssen upright in the baggage car. Its former owner had painted it dark green. Except for a few broken hammers, though, it was all right. It was kept in the hotel dining room, but I could play almost anytime, even if customers were in there. The Janssen was louder than the Rosewood. Those tall uprights with their longer bass strings can sometimes sound almost like a real grand piano. And most pianists will tell you one of the best things when the uprights came along is that they'd stay in tune for months. Square grands were notoriously hard to keep in tune, but I didn't care. My father would say, "Lord, Carrie, that piano's out of tune. How can you stand it!"

I'll tell you a secret, which I'm sure you won't believe. I think I had perfect pitch when I was a child, and I'm convinced my ears or my brain made those sour notes pitch-perfect. The Rosewood was my closest friend and it could do no wrong. I missed it so much and for so long that when I finally had the money, I tried to track it down. It went from Janesville to some people in Cedar Rapids, Iowa. That family joined the Iowa emigration to California in the early '20s and my Rosewood went with them to Modesto. I caught up with the daughter-in-law of the last-known owner, and she told me it had been sold around 1925 to a speakeasy in San Francisco, where the owners had stripped it and turned it into a liquor cabinet! She said they just loved the rosewood and mother-of-pearl inlays!

How I wish it were possible to touch that lovely instrument again! I often find it in my dreams, and awake feeling young again. Not that I ever feel old. There was a line in a book I read years ago: "Her body was kept young by constantly hurrying to keep up with her mind." Carrie Jacobs-Bond couldn't have said it better.

Not many of you today would understand how thrilled we were to be snowbound at Davis House for almost two weeks with the actor Joseph Jefferson. But if you'll substitute the name of one of your favorite movie stars — a character actor like, say, Wallace Beery or Charles Laughton — you'll get a notion of our excitement. It must have been in 1872 or '73. Mr. Jefferson was performing at the Myers Opera House in his classic drama *Rip Van Winkle*. He toured in it for years all over America, all over the world, I think. After the performances at the Opera House, Minnie would prepare a late supper for Mr. Jefferson and some of the other actors. I helped to serve and clean up. Mr. Jefferson was a man of huge appetites, with an immense figure to show for it. He spoke in a kind and careful way even after his whiskies and port, and more than once asked me to play something for him. He always spoke to me as a grown-up, not a child. "Miss Jacobs, would you be so kind as to favor us with something by Stephen Foster, or perhaps that difficult piece by Liszt you play so well." He made me feel like a woman.

After one of those wonderful grown-up evenings, I got up the courage to take a big step — one I'd been thinking about for a long time. In the years after Father died and Mother had married Mr. Williams, I was terribly lonely. I had my piano and my painting, thank heavens. But I had grown to resent my dependency on Grandfather and Minnie Davis. I needed new friends and grownup responsibilities. Now that Mr. Jefferson had made me feel like a woman, I decided to act like one. I'd get a job! I went right out an offered my services to the town milliner, Esther Strohm. She knew I was already a better-than-average seamstress and had a flair for color and design. I don't recall what she said she'd pay me — probably 50 cents a day. She said come to the shop Saturdays and every other day after school. I was so very proud of myself! I rushed to the hotel with the news.

Grandfather was anything but pleased. "You go right back and tell that Miss Strohm she's made a big mistake," he said. I'm sure I started to cry, which made matters even worse. He was near shouting at me. "I guess the men in this family will always be able to take care of the women folk." It has taken me years to accept the fact that my grandfather considered it an insult to him that I should want to have my own money. He saw it as a slap in his face. It wasn't the first time I realized this world is a man's world and that it remains so. But I have learned from many hard lessons how to make it a woman's world too. *This* woman's world at least.

On the night of the final performance of *Rip Van Winkle,* it started to snow. Minnie and I were the guests of Mr. Jefferson for the performance. It was an extra joy for both of us to see him on the Myers stage in costume and make-up, after our late-night suppers at Davis House. By then I was even more thrilled to see my favorite actor, Schneider, on the same stage. If you remember the play, Schneider is the little trained dog who plays such an important role in the first act. So he was also a regular guest at Davis House. After the first night, Grandfather and Mr. Jefferson let him sleep in my room. Even before the snowstorm, he and I had already become close friends. The play was at the Opera House for a week, and by the night of the third performance, Mr. Jefferson had to drag that sweet puppy away from me to get him to the theater on time. Then came the snow.

It turned out to be a lulu of a storm — great, sticky flakes of wet snow all night and the next day, then a deep freeze and a high wind. Drifts and sheets of ice covered the roads and the rails in every direction. Mr. Jefferson's tour was canceled, and he spent another week cooped up at the hotel. By the time the snows finally began to thaw and the *Rip Van Winkle* company was able to leave for Milwaukee, Schneider and I had become inseparable. Joseph Jefferson, that blessed man, standing ankle-deep in the slush at the depot, kissed me on the cheek and handed me Schneider's leash. "You two need each other more than old man Van Winkle does," he said. No gift has ever meant more.

I have no idea where they found another pup to replace my Schneider in the play. I can only tell you he was my constant companion for nine years. With him and my music, the vast hours of loneliness became secret treasured times of joy. He was my confidant, my friend, my critic. I told him everything and read him my favorite poems and stories. I would play and sing my new songs for him. He would listen in silence, and I swear to you, wag his tail in a certain way if he liked the song, another way if he didn't. When the Rosewood would get more than slightly out-of-tune, Schneider would bark a few times before settling down. But if we had let it go too long, he'd refuse to come into the parlor until the tuner had come and gone. He would not eat a thing unless I fed him. Other children had pets; I had Schneider.

After I was ten years old, I had refused to go to Sunday school. Grandfather didn't care. He never attended church himself. But

Minnie or Aunt Abbie would often take me to regular church services on Sunday or to prayer meetings on Wednesday nights. One night I was trying to tell the minister, Mr. Bergstrom, about Schneider, about how he had become such a happy part of my life. I must have said something like, "Schneider and I understand each other's souls." The Reverend Bergstrom took on that condescending smile that preachers must be taught in seminary. "My dear Carrie," he said, "a dog has no soul. Only humans have souls."

From that day on, the church — not God, just church — began to slip away from me. You see, I found I knew of a great truth our minister did not. On the way home I asked Minnie if she thought Schneider had a soul. "Of course he does, child. Everybody knows that," she said. I didn't tell her what Mr. Bergstrom had said. She'd have gotten after him.

When I married Edward Smith, Schneider was still with me. He had slept on my bed every night until my wedding night. From then on my new husband insisted Schneider sleep in the shed with the two hounds in Smith's family. I knew almost from the start that this was a doomed marriage, and there were many reasons. It would be unfair to claim my heartache at hearing Schneider cry in the night was one of the most telling. But it was. We fought every night over Schneider.

Within a month my precious friend died out there in the shed.

CHAPTER 7

THE ACCIDENT

If you've read my old *Roads of Melody* book, you know I didn't describe the accident that happened to me when I was eight. It was violent, and it changed my life then and forever after. If you, Dear Reader, had known of it and its aftereffects, your many kind questions about my lifelong illnesses and hospitalizations would have explained themselves. Friends ask me why I have not mentioned it in public or in print. Perhaps I was trying to pretend it had never happened. For years I fretted that I'd appear vainglorious in having overcome it. Perhaps I just didn't want your pity. My secrecy seems pointless now, twenty years later.

You know of my pride, that I overcame poverty to succeed with my music. You may have guessed that I also overcame years of almost constant pain. I can assure you that my success has rested on both the poverty and the pain. In *Roads of Melody* I told you that during my years in poverty, "...I learned much of what humanity really was." I said then and still believe, "There is only one way to know people, and that is to be as poor as you can be." If that seems self-indulgent coming from this rich old lady, I remind you that I was unable to pay my bills on time until I was over forty.

We had help at the Pleasant Avenue house. Mother had a woman to cook and clean. She lived in a cottage at a far corner of the field with our hired hand. He was a huge Swedish fellow who never once spoke to me, and I was always frightened of him. I think he was still quite young, but he was almost totally bald, had crooked brown teeth and tobacco breath and like a lot of Scandinavian men, scraggly face-hair hardly worth calling a beard. He was kind to the animals — kinder, I thought, than he was to his woman. No one was sure she was his wife — a sprightly German woman by the name of Inge. She did the housework and the farm chores that the Swede did not.

Near the house there was a small brick building once a smoke house, transformed by Mother and Inge into a playhouse for me and my friends. To this day the slightest whiff of smoked ham or fish takes me back seventy-five years to that charmed space. It was a clutter of boxes and furniture, pots and dishware and discarded grown-up clothing. For my cousin Mary and me and a few others it had become a place for imagination and endless adventure.

Mary was Aunt Abbie's only girl, three or so years older than me. She was tall for her age and not very pretty, but I heard Mother say she'd be just as comely as Aunt Abbie when she grew up. Ever since I could remember Mary had walked with a limp. I never knew what caused it, but the boys teased her about it endlessly. That's probably what drove her to books. She read everything she could get her hands on. When the rest of her class at school was still struggling through *McGuffey's Reader,* Mary was devouring Walter Scott and Louisa Alcott and even Edgar Allen Poe — considered pretty heady authors for someone her age, especially a girl. So it was Mary who dreamed up most of our smoke-house games and "happens," as she called them. One day we would be prisoners of a wicked French king, the next day, doughty pioneer women crossing the wilderness on the Oregon Trail. Sometimes we pretended to be the wise old Chippewa squaws we'd see gossiping on the far side of Rock River. I always wanted to pretend I was Jenny Lind, singing my own songs on the stage of the Myers Opera House, but Mary would have none of it.

Wisconsin summers are hot and heavy, and my mother insisted children should play outdoors in light clothing — a thin blouse usually, and some sort of knickers. We laughed and whispered and plotted the summers away until we reached my day of horror.

A few yards from the smokehouse, near the well, there was a shack where Inge, sometimes with Mother's help, did the laundry. Water was heated on an outdoor coke-fired grate, the other side of the smokehouse. It was terribly awkward and dangerous. Inge had to tote tubs of boiling water from the grate to the laundry shack. The water had to be steaming hot at Father's insistence. The world, he had announced, now knew about germs and how to slay them at 212 degrees above zero Fahrenheit.

I was playing that fateful day with Mary and several of my little girlfriends. It was a run-and-hide game, the kind children invent one day and desert the next. I was "it," and I dashed full tilt from the smokehouse into Inge's path from the grate to the laundry shack. She was hauling a full steaming tub. I saw in an instant that we would collide. I threw my arms in front of my face, of that I'm sure — so my face and hands were clear of the boiling cascade. But it flooded through my light clothing and drenched my left side, on down to my left foot and ankle. The first flash of pain was like that of extreme cold, not heat. Seconds later I could smell my flesh melting, my screams of agony mixed with Inge's of shock and terror. I ran, fast as I could run, with nowhere to go.

Just get away from here! *Make this go away*!

Inge and the Swede were the only adults there that morning. Mother was at the hotel having lunch with Aunt Abbie.

Mama will come home and make it all right.

Father had been in Racine for several days negotiating, I later learned, to get some banks and lawyers to cover his bad investments.

Father would know what to do!

I know there really isn't anything that could have been done. There still isn't, to this day. In seconds the victim undergoes third degree burns. For me they covered nearly half my entire body. Inge shrieked for help and the Swede rushed from the barn. The two of them grappled my body into the cool water of the horse-trough. I saw the Swede cower in fear and disgust as a pancake of my skin skidded into his hand. Then I must have then gone into shock and lost consciousness. I was later told that Inge, wisely my father said, ran to the kitchen and returned with a tub of lard. She and the Swede stripped me and spread it all over my body. Then they wrapped me in clean muslin and the two of them carried me into my bedroom.

The next two months were a blur of exhaustion and pain. Father, telegraphed in Racine, raced home. He summoned Dr. D.W. Bond, and also Dr. Palmer, his Civil War commandant. All three agreed there wasn't much anyone could do. The body had to heal as best it could, the patient made as comfortable as possible during the process. Dr. Palmer, who had probably treated far more baneful burn wounds than the others, told me years later that he feared for my life. For days, he said, he had to fend off the silent hope that death might indeed occur.

Dr. Palmer was a kind enough man, but affected gruffness, I suppose to distance himself from the miseries he confronted day after day. He had come home to Janesville a Civil War hero — a loud, barrel-chest of a man sporting the bushy mustache and mutton-chops so fashionable then. I knew from Father the horrors his big, bony hands had touched, but they were warm hands, always gentle when they touched my spoiled flesh. Dr. Palmer maintained his practice in Janesville even during his years as Wisconsin Surgeon General up in Madison, so I spent months in his care as a recovering youngster and then a young adult. He warned me that burns as deep as mine would cause permanent damage to my nervous system. "But your scars, Carrie," he said, "will build up some protection as the years pass."

One day when I'd come in for some drugs and lotions, he looked at my back and shoulders where the lesions were the worst and said, "Carrie Jacobs, that burn should have killed you. It probably would have killed someone twice your age and size." He shook his head. "I'm astonished at your will to live. Doctors wish they could bottle that power for others. But it's either in your bones or it isn't. You are a survivor, my dear."

Yes, dear Dr. Palmer, and I still am. The body you saw so brutally damaged has passed through eighty-three years on this earth. The legacy of that dread moment has, as you warned me, triggered breakdowns and long episodes of distress and torment that have brought me close to death — several times uninvited, other times devoutly wished for.

My parents, Grandfather, Minnie, Aunt Abbie — all of them pitched in to help me through. Salves and powders were lovingly applied, stories and poems read over and over, puzzles and games were offered, it seemed, every hour. Minnie taught me to play pinochle. I'm quite certain I would not have survived without this endless love, to which I am ever indebted.

If I had known that within six months after the accident I'd be standing at my father's grave, I might have given up and gone ahead so I'd be waiting for him in Heaven. He loved me enough to force me, through my pain, back to the piano. Barely a month after the accident he carried me there. "Play, Carrie," he said. Every day it was, "Sit up and play. Sing to me, precious." The scarring had attacked my posture. "*Sit up straight, my darling*. I know it hurts you. Play for me." I did, for hours at a time. I played through my tears, and his. I played and sang my own melodies and every piece he and Mother brought me. I decided music was somehow a reward for my suffering and an unfailing escape from it. I came to believe the trials I survived gave me the grit to beat back every challenge the world could hand me from then on.

"Play, Carrie. Sit up straight and play."

Myers Opera House had just opened in Janesville. It was 1870. Father and Mother took me to a concert there, my first real outing since the accident.

The artist was Blind Tom.

CHAPTER 8

BLIND IDOLS

The story in *Roads of Melody* of my meeting Blind Tom is true, as far as it goes. But I want to add certain lifelong reflections about it. I was eight years old and was already quite a pianist — "by ear." I could play anything I heard, my greatest triumph being Liszt's *Second Hungarian Rhapsody*, a popular chestnut then and now. Unable yet to read music, I still mastered it note for note from hearing Mr. Titcomb play it at school.

It was 1870, just a few weeks before Father's death. He and Mother took me to the brand-new Myers Opera House in Janesville to see Blind Tom. I still have the program for that evening. It explained how Tom was the son of a slave woman in Georgia, born blind. They soon realized he was also an "imbecile" — a hateful word, but proper I suppose in those pre-Freudian times. But Tom was also born with a gift — the one I knew I too possessed — the ability to hear and play back in detail any piece of music. Tom's gift was of course a thousand-fold more grand and powerful than mine. According to the program he had begun as a toddler to imitate the sounds of nature — everything he heard — wind and thunder, horses and dogs, birds, crickets. Then he discovered a piano. It was in the home of his mother's master, a Mr. Bethune. He went to the keyboard and played with total accuracy a piece he had heard the master's daughter play earlier in the day.

Some of you may recall stories in the newspapers about Blind Tom, though now long ago. Tom died in 1908, and I don't think he had appeared in public for some time, but for thirty years or more he was a great celebrity, touring the opera houses and concert halls of America and Europe under the management of the Bethune family. It's said they amassed a fortune from his career. I had guessed that Tom was in his mid-thirties that night in Janesville, but I realize now he was much younger, perhaps twenty or twenty-one. They had put him on tour when he was barely ten, so he was already a much-talked-about attraction when he came to our town.

He was sad to behold — overweight, ungainly, given to whirling around and slapping himself, uttering guttural sounds one moment, bird calls and whistles the next. But his playing! It was astonishing. He executed a few of the classics including my cherished Liszt Rhapsody, and some of his own compositions. Then came the main event. As was the custom, Tom's manager had invited a local musician to compose something that Tom would hear for the first time. Our Mr. Titcomb, (soon to be my piano teacher), had written a piece just for the occasion. He played it once through for Tom, who lurched 'round the stage all the while, smacking his lips and grunting. Then this miraculous blind musician sat down and played Mr. Titcomb's piece note for note. Not a mistake, and I knew for certain! Remember — in those days my own ear retained every note of every piece I heard.

One of our town drunkards had climbed onto the stage while Mr. Titcomb was playing his challenge piece and struck a discordant note in the treble, grinning like a fool to the audience as if to say, "Let him play that!!" I recall crying in anger at the man. But when Blind Tom arrived at that point, both his hands occupied with the difficulties of the piece itself, he leaned over casually and struck the naughty note *with his nose!* The audience went wild. I was dumbstruck. I thought Blind Tom the most wonderful man in the world.

Now someone shouted "We have a girl in our town that can do the same thing. Little Carrie Jacobs. Get her up there!" You might expect me to have begged off, shy and fearful, but I was excited and totally confidant — a confidence I wish I might have preserved in my life to come. My mother and father walked me to the stage, where Blind Tom proceeded to play a fiery piece — a march of his own composition. I won't say I played it back note-perfect but I was pretty close, and this time the house really came down.

I can still play that march. I cannot explain this. I shared a gift with Blind Tom, his gift far more profound than mine, surely, but a gift in common. A blind colored man born in slavery and deemed an idiot bonded with an eight-year-old white child from a village in Wisconsin. Father, revisiting his education as a physician, discussed the evening endlessly with Mother and with his friends, especially Dr. D.W. Bond, Frank's father. Both were men of quick and curious mind, galvanized by the event, desperate to find a scientific basis for this "miracle." Some people have speculated that Blind Tom was guided by the spirit world. Father would have none of that. He was, Mother said, agnostic on such matters, and was not a church-going man. Nor indeed was Grandfather Davis. My mother spoke of God every day of her life, but seldom went to church — this in a day when church membership was assumed of every good citizen.

My own childhood memories of our random visits to the Presbyterian Church remind me only of how boring I found their hymns and how sterile I found the meeting hall they called a church. With a friend I would occasionally attend Janesville's little Catholic Church. I feasted on the glowing colors and bright garments I saw there, although I couldn't understand a word of the service. Then, when I was thirteen and studying music with Mr. Titcomb, I played the organ for his choir at the First Unitarian Church. I didn't understand all of their beliefs, but I liked their rejection of the Trinity because I had also been wrestling with it. Ralph Waldo Emerson's theories about Transcendentalism were all the talk at the Unitarian meetings — pretty boring, I thought, as was their music. But Emerson led me to poetry: — his and Whitman's and Wordsworth's. I read Elizabeth Barrett Browning and later on, Emily Dickinson. Poetry has taught me more about the presence of the divine in my life that any church sermon, or even the Bible itself. It may surprise you, but I believe the motley connections to God in my childhood are the very thing that brought me in later life a certainty of God's grace, a certainty that has guided my life and infuses my music. I don't go to church and haven't for years. But God is in my life every day.

You may wonder why the inspiration of Blind Tom didn't launch little Carrie Jacobs into a career as a concert pianist, but of course it did not. Father died a few months later. Given his curiosity, he might have thought it best for me to develop my personal gift for a while longer. But my mother and my grandfather Davis soon decided piano lessons were a must. It wasn't long after my first lesson with Mr.Titcomb that I felt my gift slipping away — my ability to listen, retain the notes, and play them all back. I can still play "by ear" of course, in the manner of most professionals. But the concert stage was clearly not in my future. I was a good girl and practiced hard, but scales and Czerny exercises never came easily. I had my own fingering. I could play all the trills and runs, but I was angry when I had to learn *their* way of doing them.

So my childhood gift faded. But I never forgot that night with Blind Tom. I didn't see him ever again, but occasionally I'd notice his appearing nearby — twice in Chicago after Frank Bond died. By then I had neither the will nor the money to buy a ticket. I dwelt often on that dramatic night with Tom in Janesville, but I lost track of him until I met, years later, his successor — a similar genius, the man they called Blind Boone. He appeared in 1913 or so at the Auditorium Theater in Chicago. This time I had both the money and a deep desire to attend. The house was packed.

He opened with some gracious and humorous remarks and then proceeded to execute the same "trick" that Blind Tom had originated, playing back note for note, compositions brought to the stage by the cream of Chicago musicians. But while Blind Tom was viewed, sadly, as a freak due to his primitive antics and garbled speech, Mr. Boone was a polished raconteur as well as a superb artist, a handsome man of elegant manner, sumptuously dressed. After he had paraded his memory tricks to everyone's awe and applause, he then undertook some classics by the likes of Chopin and Lizst, playing them to perfection. When he came back after the intermission, he said something like "Now let's have some cookies," and launched into his arrangements of folk songs, popular tunes, and a bit of the ragtime, so much a craze at the time.

I hurried backstage to meet him. He bowed formally, reached for my hand and told me how he loved my songs — that if he'd known I was in the audience he would have performed them in his own style. He introduced me to his gracious wife and to his manager, a Mr. Lang. I invited them to come by the Bond Shop next day for lunch or tea. John

William Boone and I thus became friends until his death in 1927, a friendship sealed when we found we shared a life-changing experience. I was too shy at first to divulge to him my childhood meeting with Blind Tom. Perhaps I should not have been surprised when he told me of his.

John William Boone was about my age. He had not been a slave, but was born in Missouri to a mother who was a runaway. He was not born blind, as was Blind Tom Bethune, but as an infant he had developed a deadly fever or disease. Thinking to save the child's life, a "doctor" chose to remove his eyes, then sewed shut his lids. Ghastly as it sounds, the little fellow did survive, and soon, as a toddler, repeated Blind Tom's adventure in hearing the "white folks" play something on a piano and repeating it precisely. I believe he then received some instruction off and on, but was thrown into terrible hardship growing up. As he sought help and understanding he found himself arrested as a runaway vagabond on the streets of St. Louis. He suffered unspeakable humiliation at the hand of various promoters who paraded his talents in saloons and brothels, until finally he found a loyal friend and benefactor, the Mr. Lang I met years later.

Mr. Boone explained that when he was sixteen, still in Missouri, he was taken to hear Blind Tom. That would have been perhaps ten years after my night with Tom. As I pictured these two sightless giants joining in music on that long ago day, I began to weep, and lay my head on Boone's massive shoulder as he poured out the same story I myself had re-lived ever since childhood. Tom had done his miracles, someone in the audience had shouted "Listen to our boy Blind Boone. He can do the same thing!" And it happened just as it had with me. The happy result was that Boone, the hard homeless years behind him, was brought into disciplined musical training at a college in Missouri and emerged as a full-fledged concert artist.

We met occasionally after that first day, and I saw Mr. Boone often enough to discuss "the gift" with him. How, given the added burden (or could it possibly be the *advantage)* of blindness, did he and Tom somehow turn the piano into an extension of their own flesh? This despite the fact that a piano is a cold, uncaring construction, a machine. How can flesh and spirit connect?

We agreed. We had no idea.

I wish both Boone and Bethune could have heard Art Tatum play the piano. I hope he's known to you — a negro, also blind. I was taken to hear him play several times at the Three Deuces nightclub in Chicago. Mr. Tatum has not, as far as I know, ever displayed the gift of retention, as have the others. But his playing is astonishing, other-worldly. It's called jazz I suppose, but it hardly resembles other music these days that goes by that name. He'll play a well-known popular song like Vincent Youmans's *Tea for Two,* and then sail off into stunning improvisations and variations I find unimaginable. I pride myself on a good sense of harmony, and can usually track the chord progressions in music as I listen. But with him I cannot. His is another world. I was introduced to him by friends and we had a quick chat once, but I've never had the opportunity to talk with him about that mysterious connection of fingers and keyboard.

I have, by the way, often discussed it with dear Alec Templeton, that brilliant pianist and writer, an Englishman (he insists Welsh) — a funny fellow whose satiric monologues have made him a radio favorite. Alec has been blind since birth. Bless his heart, he telephoned me a few years ago — we had never met — and said "Mrs. Bond, I have your telephone number from Gus Haenschen, the conductor for NBC's American Album of Familiar Music. He reminded me you live here in California and said 'You must call her.'" I had heard Alec play at one of our Hollywood Bowl concerts and admired his command of the piano, not to mention his wonderful sense of humor. I said how nice it was to hear from him, but why this particular day? He said "Listen in to NBC tonight at 8 o'clock." I did of course, and that sweet man played a medley of my three so-called "hits," played them exquisitely. We became friends, and talked often about the enigmas of music and musicians. He had not been born with the gift, and quizzed me endlessly about it, and about his brothers in blindness. He hated bigotry in any form. I was with him when we first heard the big Count Basie Orchestra in Santa Monica. As we were leaving one of Alec's assistants said something like, "Not bad, considering he's a colored man." (But that's not the term the man used.) Alec was furious. "Is he really?" he shot back. "I hadn't noticed."

CHAPTER 9

FRANZ LISZT AND FRANK BOND

I was in the second grade when I heard Mr. Titcomb play Liszt's *Hungarian Rhapsody #2.* There was some sort of recital. It wouldn't have been in church, so it must have been at school. I didn't pay much attention. The room was noisy. Boys were shooting spitwads and shuffling their feet, so I couldn't really hear it. But I fell in love with it a few weeks later. Mr. Titcomb would often come to our house on Pleasant Street for Sunday dinner. He could hardly wait for Mother to ask if he'd go to the Rosewood and play something for us. Father played the flute passing well, and if Dr. D.W. Bond and his wife Jane were in town, they'd bring along cello and violin. Our miniature musicales became the talk of the town.

I can remember to this day — when I heard Liszt in the quiet of our parlor —how it thrilled me. I shivered. My whole body seemed to dance. I *had* to play it. As soon as the grownups left I went straight to the piano. By now I was playing quite well — way beyond just picking out tunes with one hand. I was yet to take my first formal piano lesson, and my fingering must have been of my own devising, but I was playing well, with both hands. I could *see* the music dancing above my fingers. I don't mean I saw notes on a staff. I didn't know about them yet. I saw the music — in my own way. It was my own invention, my secret.

I loved the whole piece, but it was the main section that I mastered right away — the part I learned later that Liszt called *giusto vivace.* Everyone knows it — dah-dah-dah-DAH, da-dah-dah-DAH — on it goes, measure after measure — that same irresistible figure. I played the whole piece in my own key, which turned out to be the key of F — one flat. I don't think I saw a printed copy of the music until years later, when dear Gustav Schirmer sent me a birthday copy from their files. I was gratified to discover that Liszt had played the *giusto vivace* in my key! After I had learned about music and harmony I found that he'd scored other sections of the piece in different keys, but I kept on playing the whole thing in F — still do. Even that dark and dramatic opening part, which he wrote in C minor (three flats), I played in D minor — still one flat, like my major key of F. I didn't know yet that musicians called it the relative minor. Somehow my ear just took me there.

Much as I loved the Liszt *Rhapsody* for its own sake, it came later to play a role in my falling in love with Frank Bond. I was only fourteen, but the grownups were right when they noticed I was "very advanced for my age." Frank Bond was my first real date. He was eighteen. The Bonds lived in nearby Johnstown Center. His father D.W. Bond, being a doctor same as mine, meant that the Bonds and the Jacobs's had become good friends before Father's death and would remain so. I started to flirt with Frank when he was fourteen or fifteen and I was ten or eleven. At that age four years is an unbridgeable gap, but I knew all along that Frank Bond was the "cat's meow," as we used to say.

The Myers Opera House had opened in January of 1870 and had been the scene of my enchanted meeting with Blind Tom. I suppose because Janesville was on the route from Chicago to Madison, many fine artists began stopping off to present a concert at the Myers. We seldom had the money to go, but then it was announced that Julia Reeve King was coming to town. She was quite famous as I recall, at least in the Middle West. Her selections were to include Liszt's *Hungarian Rhapsody #2!*

I have no idea to this day how my "date" for the concert with Frank Bond came about. Did he offer to take the Jacobs girl out of courtesy to the family? Was it simply coincidence or fate or serendipity? I doubt it. I think it may have been a long-range match-making scheme of my mother's to bring another physician into the family. Frank Bond was now a man of eighteen. And so dashing! He had already grown his mustache. He was a student at Milton College and was planning on Rush Medical in Chicago.

It was a real date. We had no chaperone. I wore one of Aunt Abbie's gowns. Frank came to the hotel for me in a rented chaise. I was in heaven. The Opera House was elegant. I don't suppose it would seem very much by today's standards, but it seated almost 200 people. It had four boxes and an orchestra pit. For years after, in my dreams of that evening, the whole Opera House was done up in red plush. There was a gaslight chandelier, and when the concert began and Miss King made her entrance, they brought her on stage in limelight.

It was one of the first concerts of the season at the Myers, and the town dressed up fit to kill to welcome Julia Reeves King. Dr. Bond (D.W.) and Jane were there in evening clothes, tactfully seated nowhere near us. Mother and her husband said they couldn't get over from Milton because the weather was turning bad, but I like to think my wise Mama didn't want to hover and cramp my style with Frank Bond.

I don't remember exactly what Miss King played in the first part of her concert — a few waltzes by Chopin, I think. Then something by Louis Moreau Gottschalk which I didn't care for at all. She was dressed in a light blue taffeta gown with silly ruffles and a high neck which disappointed my 14-year-old visions of concert glamour. But when she came back after the Intermission she had changed into a severe black gown of velvet or velour, with a necklace of pearls set against its daring exposure of her lovely neck and shoulders. She began with the *Rhapsody*. She played it perfectly, of course.

I fell in love all over again for Franz Liszt. I fell in love with Julia Reeve King. And I'm quite sure on that night, in that sublime moment, I fell forever in love with Frank Bond. I wish we could have gotten married the next day — at that age. People today forget how much earlier boys and girls matured in those days. We had to. I may have been only fourteen, but I can tell you that Carrie Jacobs's fourteen years on this earth had produced a very mature and fully-developed female. I didn't know much about the details yet, but I knew I was ready to live with a man.

CHAPTER 10

DR. BOND AND MR. SMITH

My eighteenth birthday came and went on August 11th of 1880 without much of a party. Minnie made me one her special devil's food cakes. Frank Bond wasn't free to come down from Iron River. Cousin Mary came by Davis House with a small gift. Two girl friends from my high school class marched their new husbands in for tea, and let me know that a dozen other classmates we planning weddings in the fall. Late in the afternoon Mary's ex-beau Edward Smith made an appearance, and we thought he would never leave. It was my first hint that Edward, spurned by Mary, intended now to court her cousin Carrie.

My days were spent in longing for two things: the love of Frank Bond and success of some kind for my music. In the weeks since graduation I was busy but unsatisfied. I was working afternoons at Miss Strohm's millinery shop, and I had a tiny income embroidering and painting china. I had taken on a few piano students and was playing the organ at the Methodist Church. The melodies in my head gave me no rest. More than ever I dreamed my childhood dream of writing songs. It seemed to this young woman, at this disturbing time, a dream fast fading.

Mother was busy settling into her third marriage. At least it had brought her back to Janesville, and she managed an evening or two with me at the hotel in late August. She fretted about my future, and badgered me a bit too much about my prospects for marriage. I told her I was seeing two fellows, one seriously. She had of course known Frank Bond since he was a child. She knew little about Edward Smith beyond some gossip from Aunt Abbie. Edward Smith, I assured her, was just a friend. Mother clearly hoped I would marry Frank Bond. He was going to be a physician, and that was important to her because of Father.

A few weeks later she said to me, "Don't be foolish, Carrie Jacobs. Frank Bond will make you a fine husband. He's finishing his medical training over in Chicago. As a doctor he'll understand and accept your condition, far better than that Smith fellow." By my "condition" she clearly meant the limitations and pain the accident had imposed on my body.

"Young Smith seems nice enough," she said, "but he strikes me as a bit of a ne'er-do-well, without much in the way of a future. You just wait. I'm betting when young Doctor Bond gets back to Janesville, he'll pop the question."

He did not.

How the passage of time changes us! This old lady must now revisit her 18-year-old self and try to remember who she was, then. She can easily now revisit the seven blissful years after she finally did become Mrs. Frank Bond, however sadly they ended. And she can dutifully relive the eight dull years of waiting for him, knowing now that her dream of love would one day finally arrive. But her younger self saw only the end of hope. A lovely Wisconsin autumn promising great joy changed in one day to a time of sorrow and shame.

Frank Bond did finish at Rush Medical, and he did return to Janesville, only to leave a few months later to join his father in Iron River. D.W. Bond was moving his medical practice and his pharmacy to that primitive town. Frank Bond had little choice but to follow. He had been promised a partnership in D.W.'s practice. I don't think

Frank had any notion that the real goal of his father was to make a lot of money in the iron mines up there.

But father and son were still making frequent trips back and forth, and Frank never failed to call on me at Davis House. We would often dine together, take long walks, twice attending concerts at the Myers Opera House. You may be sure those concerts were a special treasure, reminding me of the 14-year-old who a few years before had fallen in love with her "older man." She was now a woman. And more in love than ever.

I wish I could show you a picture of Frank Bond in those days. The only one I have was taken when he was 36, the year before he died. He looks very stern and serious, and indeed could be both. But he was still cheerful and full of life. At twenty-two those very traits literally defined him. Everybody loved Frank Bond. He seemed born to become a trusted physician. He had big smooth hands with beautiful nails that were always trimmed and clean. His voice had deepened into a calm baritone that would soothe many a frightened patient in the years ahead. He had grown the mandatory mustache as soon as his glands made it possible, but he kept the rest of his face hairless all his life. He sported no mutton chops, no goatee like his father. Of course I thought him the most handsome fellow in Wisconsin. If I had to use just one word to describe him, I'd choose "vital." That was the quality that made him irresistible to me.

Frank Bond asked me to go up to Madison with him for Thanksgiving. He had two friends from Rush Medical working there. We took lodging in a hotel, with separate rooms. After a glorious evening of music and good food and laughter, we stayed together until the morning. I don't know how else to say it. After that we were inseparable. I took the last train home on Sunday. Frank went back to Iron River early the next day.

I saw my mother a few days later, and I gave nothing away except to tell her I was, as they would say today, "gaga" about Frank Bond. That wise woman saw beyond my rapture, and a day or two later this letter came from her. Her knowledge and advice about men were to serve me well, but not before eight dreary years had passed.

November 26, 1880

Dearest Carrie:

You must understand, my dear daughter, that in private moments with your new husband, his needs will dominate. I have come to think of those needs as an arc — the arc of his pleasure. He will reach the top of the arc very quickly in the early days of your marriage, perhaps with such urgency that it will frighten you. Then, almost as rapidly, he will come back down to earth, so to speak.

Women are given to believe that we do not possess a similar arc of pleasure. We are taught simply to go along best we can at these times, not only out of love and respect for our husbands, but because we know a tiny new life may begin within us. But some of us discover our own needs. We find that we too have an arc of pleasure, ours rising and falling slowly and more quietly than his, but every bit as sweet and joyful. Perhaps even more so.

I'm sorry to say that most women never find this in themselves. But I did, when I was younger than you are now. I can tell you that your Aunt Abbie and I knew things — things found out in secret times together. Perhaps you have already found your own way, as we did. If not I can only assure you that it is there to be revealed to you.

Most men don't know about this — perhaps don't care to know. Many of them, poor boys, are brought up to see only shame and disgust. At quite an early age some are initiated by way of a few frantic minutes with a prostitute. Your father told me some of his friends considered it their duty to arrange such a sullied visit for their sons, often at the first signs of their manhood. Other men come to marriage as unversed as their brides. Lots of them continually boast and joke, your father often said, to hide their ignorance or fear, or both. In either case they are young, Carrie, so very young. You must remember that in youth, a man's arc is a steep one. Try as you will to share it, it belongs to him, and he is desperate to ascend and complete it. I do hope you'll also remember this. These needs of a young man make themselves known insistently to him many times a day, in a manner that has no counterpart in us.

I was seventeen when I married your father — a year younger than you are now. He was twenty-one, just out of the Albany Medical School up in New York. Oh my dear, he was so handsome, and such fun. What I want you to know is that Dr. Jacobs saw to my needs as well as his own. Whether his medical knowledge led to this, I don't know. I doubt it. I find most physicians possess no more ardor or understanding that other men. A loving husband, dear Carrie, is a husband who *understands* — listen to me closely — who understands *your* need in the intimate hours together. This man will rest a bit and then revisit you. You'll find now the frenzy of his needs will have gentled and slowed, and on the best of days, matching yours.

Dear Carrie, no man has ever held me and helped me like your sainted father. My Mr. Williams was very shy — kind-hearted but distant. You must surely wonder why I would marry again so soon after losing him so suddenly. I can only tell you that at this stage of my life, I intend to go on seeking the kind of love your father brought to me. I may never find it again. But I shall try.

Your affectionate,
Mother

In mid-December I telegraphed Frank Bond that I was quite certain we must be married, and soon. He came to Janesville two days later. He insisted that he loved me, but that marriage was out of the question right now. It was not the time, he said, for me to join him in the primitive settlements up North, and he and his father had no intention of returning to Janesville. He suggested how we must otherwise "work this out for now."

I just couldn't. I told him so.

He left the next morning. I didn't sleep for three days, and experienced the first episode of vicious headache and pain in my leg and shoulders that would recur the rest of my life, a punishment I can only believe a breaking heart impinged on my scarred body.

I hated Frank Bond. And I still loved him.

Edward Smith had also grown up in Johnstown Center, Frank Bond's hometown. He was a sweet boy, very quiet. He was not very ambitious. I don't think he finished the eighth grade, but then neither did many working class and farm children. Edward always had a job. I can't remember a day when he wouldn't say, "I've got money. I've got plenty of money." He was a big man, red-faced and near-sighted. He lacked any sense of the artistic, didn't sing, even in church. At fifteen or so, he seemed a grown man, and was courting my Cousin Mary in his clumsy fashion. Mary, just as Mother had predicted, had become quite pretty. Instead of hiding her game leg (I think it must have been from polio, although we'd never heard of it then), she had made the limp her trademark. She was ever so cute and clever, and could trigger laughter in a crowd or party like no one else. Poor Edward Smith was head over heels in love with her. But when Mary went over to Milwaukee to become a teacher, he gave up the chase.

I had become something of a friend-in-need to him after he saw he had no chance of Mary's affection. The more he cried on my shoulder about her, the more clearly I saw that he was desperate for love. I didn't want him transferring that desperation to me. My heart belonged to Frank Bond. Edward Smith knew it, and didn't seem bothered playing second fiddle. In the weeks that followed he came often by the hotel. I made no secret of my feelings for Frank Bond, but on days of mutual loneliness Edward and I would lunch or picnic together. I suppose he saw it as a courtship. A time or two after Mary went off to Milwaukee, he'd say, "I just love you, Carrie Jacobs, I just do." And I'd say, "Yes, Edward, I'm your best pal and I love you, too." I didn't mean *love!*

My anguish over Frank Bond finally gave way to sleep. I slept for a full day and night. I awoke to a crisp December day knowing I still loved him and always would, proud that I was carrying his child, vowing that someday, somehow, we'd be together.

Edward Smith, needy as ever, called on me the next day. I said nothing about Frank Bond, but I suppose in his own loneliness, my frightened, broken heart lay transparent to him.

Edward Smith and I were married on December 28, 1880. My son was born the following July.

CHAPTER 11

CARRIE JACOBS SMITH

The secrets here have gone to the grave with everyone but me, and I'll be there before much longer. I am eighty-three years old. I find my strength and my will ebbing day by day. The effort to write is becoming unbearable. It's important to get this chapter on the page.

Edward had wanted us to wait until spring to get married, but I knew there was no time for a long engagement. A few nights later we were at my mother's. Members of her new family, the Minors, were gathered around, along with aunt Abby Ford and Mary and the others. Barely six weeks had past since my tryst with Frank Bond in Madison, but I knew I was going to have a baby. I sensed that Mother knew, but her cheerful nature took over.

"Carrie! Why don't you and Edward have a Christmas wedding? That way," she laughed, "he'll never forget your anniversary!" The mood was a pretended lark for Mother and me, but Edward seemed truly happy. He told us, "I'm the luckiest man in all Wisconsin. I'm marrying the girl of my dreams." My luckiest years were yet to come as the wife of Dr. Frank Bond, but I couldn't have dreamed it then.

How could I? Not that my affection for Edward at the time wasn't sincere, but it was nothing like the overwhelming longing in my heart for Frank. Edward, on the other hand, was slavishly adoring.

He worked around Janesville in clothing and shoe stores the first two years of our marriage with little sign of advancement. When my uncle George Davis in Chicago offered to train Edward in the tailor's trade — "cutting" as he called it — we bundled up our belongings and moved over there. Within less than a year I knew it had been a mistake. Worse, I realized that whatever tie that had existed between my husband and me was slipping away. I was earning a little money — supporting us, really, with my painting and designing. I was even offered a steady job with a wholesaler there in Chicago. Edward, on the other hand, turned out to have no talent or ambition for the new trade and was a hopeless apprentice. He found Uncle George mean and surly, became blue and discouraged, felt himself a failure, and feared he would never again have money of his own. I did a foolish thing that Christmas, our third anniversary. I borrowed money from Uncle and presented Edward with seventy-five gold dollars on a dinner plate. He didn't say a word, just slid them into his coat pocket and walked out. He came home late that night, and for the first time I saw he'd been drinking.

Both of us sullen and distant, we left our things in Chicago and moved back to Janesville, whereupon I became terribly ill. It was the worst onset yet of the attacks that would plague me off and on the rest of my life. I went to Dr. Palmer, the dear man who had seen me through the accident of my childhood. He said he was not surprised, that what he called my "neuroma" was triggered by severe nerve damage which might be with me all my life. He sent me to the hospital in Madison. I was there for three months. Mother and the Minor family, thank God, took care of my little three-year-old.

My life had become a nightmare. Edward's self-esteem, low to begin with, collapsed further with his drinking. We lived in a series of rooming houses in Janesville and Milton, and he would often be gone for days at a time. Friends whispered that he was seeing other women. I begged him for the truth. "Just deny it," I pleaded with him. "Deny it, dear Edward, and I will believe you." He refused to say anything, but I knew it was true.

Forgive me for what I'm going to tell you now. I feel I'm writing for one of those awful "true confession" magazines. I began to see Frank Bond again.

After those last dreadful weeks in 1880 leading to my Christmas Day marriage, they said around Janesville that Frank, too, had gotten married — "a woman up north somewhere." It wasn't so. Letters from Frank began to reach me soon after my marriage, addressed in his fine Spencerian hand, in care of mother or Minnie at the hotel.

> April 20, 1881
>
> My darling Carrie,
>
> I don't know how to begin this letter, except first to beg for your forgiveness. My conduct last fall was unprincipled and shameful. I pray for your health and safety as you await the birth of the child. Our child. I can only wish that your marriage to Edward brings you the measure of happiness that you so richly deserve, and that he will be a kind father to the child and a good provider for both of you.
>
> I need to tell you that I have not married. I had intended to do so after you and I parted last December, and I began seeing a woman here in Iron River. It was simply not to be. She is a worthy enough person, but I found I could not make a lifetime commitment to her. My every thought and prayer these days go out to you, with regret and shame that my commitment was not made to you, dear Carrie, as surely it should have been.
>
> Perhaps the ache in my heart will pass with the coming years. For now I shall commit myself only to the demands of this hard frontier village for a physician's care, and in moments left to myself, pray for your forgiveness. If there is any love left in your heart for me, perhaps, if the pain should ease, we might see each other again.
>
> Your loving,
> Frank Bond.

This was my reply.

May 5, 1881
Dear Dr. Bond,
Are you trying to break my heart yet again? I have no desire to see you. Please do not write again for any reason.
Carrie Jacobs Smith

But he did write again — a few weeks after Frederic was born July 23rd.

August 19, 1881
Dearest Carrie,
Please let me into your life long enough to express how thankful I am for the safe delivery of baby Frederic. I can only conclude that my father had no idea that he was a party to the birth of his grandson. I'm pleased that he just happened to be in Janesville the week of Frederic's birth, if the services of a physician should have been necessary. He reported that the attentions of Mrs. Flannery and her daughter, with your mother standing by, were quite sufficient.
I shall be in Janesville in September and would welcome an invitation to see little Frederic (and his Mama) if that's possible.
As always,
Frank Bond

I was still too shattered to even think of it.

August 30, 1881
Dear Dr. Bond,
I can hardly refuse your wish to see baby Frederic, and suggest on your trip to Janesville you arrange a visit through my mother, Mrs. James D. Minor.
Sincerely,
Carrie Smith

Almost two years went by.

After Edward and I had returned from our year in Chicago and I fell so badly ill, Frank wrote to me at the hospital in Madison. These are the last of many letters that I'll share with you. They foreshadow what will come.

> March 18, 1884
> My Darling Carrie,
> On a recent trip to Janesville, I visited your mother. She was gracious as always and introduced me to young master Frederic Smith. Except for his colicky tummy, he seems as fine a three-year-old as the whole state of Wisconsin has to offer. She informed me that you had been severely ill, and urged that I consult Dr. Palmer about your condition and your whereabouts in Madison. I shall be in that city later this month. Please grant me the privilege of a brief visit.
> With affection always,
> Frank

My reply was written from my hospital bed.

> March 29, 1884
> Dearest Frank,
> Please come.
> My endeavors in Chicago with Edward came to naught. Our belongings are still there, he has provided no place for me after I leave the hospital. I am in mounting dismay about the future for myself and little Frederic.
> Please come.
> Carrie

And he did come. The hospital was just a few blocks from the hotel where he and I had spent our Thanksgiving weekend only a few years before. He urged me to leave Edward Smith and leave Janesville and go with him then and there to Iron River, but we drew back from that, knowing it would only compound our sins. So we waited.

I saw Frank Bond many times after that. Another year passed. Early in 1885 Frank wrote that he'd heard about a job for a woman up in Marinette, Wisconsin — a governess of sorts who could teach art and music. (The divorce papers say it was Marquette, way up in Michigan. A mistake, but what does it matter now? It did matter then. Marinette was an easy trip from Iron River because the railroad had gone through.) I went to Marinette and stayed six months. Frank and I were together many times.

And I found I was to have another child.

Edward and I had not been together for months. There was no choice, and I agreed with Frank that this time we would have to "do something about it." We took the train to Milwaukee and saw a doctor Frank had known from Rush Medical. A few days later I went back to Janesville. My relief was mixed with mourning for my lost child and my guilt over an added betrayal of Edward. Sometimes I suffer still, and must write that I felt a divine punishment was brought on me. Down through the years my family and friends have asked gently why Edward and I had had no more children. Even more painful, why didn't Frank and I provide Frederic with a little brother or sister during the seven years of our own marriage?

I couldn't. After Milwaukee I found I was no longer able to bear a child.

How could I blame Edward for our distress and separation? He must have known I was "carrying a torch" for Frank Bond. And why wouldn't he need other women? After our first few years of awkward tenderness, he and I were no longer intimate. Early in our marriage he had accepted the limitations wrought on my body from the accident. He was quite dear about it, and we found ways to please each other. But as his other anxieties and fears grew, this problem somehow added to his doubts about himself. Frank Bond, on the other hand, was so much more worldly than poor Edward. That fact, along with a doctor's recognition of my needs and the remembered delicacy of our courtship and first fulfillment, led us at last into a world of love I had never dreamed possible.

Edward Smith chose not to appear in Rock County District Court when I sought a divorce on grounds of non-support. We started in October of 1888 and ended with the final decree on December 8th. No attorney represented him. My attorney, Mr. Nolan, told the court that Edward said "...he just wanted to get rid of me." And he said the defendant had admitted that "...he hadn't really treated his wife right, and didn't blame her." I had to fight back the tears when Edward added, according to Mr. Nolan, that "...he imagined Carrie had never loved him, and that was probably why he hadn't treated her better."

I told the court how difficult life had become, what with Edward's drinking and carousing. I testified that Edward had come to constantly cursing me, and how once he made little Frederic listen while he cursed and abused me in a drunken tantrum. The judge said they should strike that from the record because I wasn't suing "for cruelty, but for failure to support," but Mr. Nolan insisted it stay in — that it would make a difference on how the court decided alimony and child support. The verdict was that I would get custody of Frederic and Edward was to pay one hundred dollars per year — $25.00 every three months until Frederic was eighteen.

At the end, God forgive me, I said, "He was a very kind husband for three years. I loved him with all my heart, but now I haven't a particle of love for him." What I couldn't say was I had loved Frank Bond with all my heart all those years, and that my final day in court was probably the happiest in eight long years of marriage.

You can well imagine how the tongues wagged in Janesville. Divorces may be a dime a dozen these days, especially here in Hollywood, but not in 1888 in Janesville. That nice Jacobs girl? People just didn't get divorced, no matter how miserable their marriages turned out to be. Years later I saw a wonderful remark by my Chicago friend Finley Peter Dunne in one of his Mister Dooley stories. In those days, he said, "A couple that found that it was impossible to go on living together — went on living together."

Frank Bond and I were married in Racine on June 9th the following year, after waiting a "proper" six months. But I had stolen up to see him several times during the long winter. Seven-year-old Frederic and I stayed in Janesville with Mother and Mr. Minor. I think Mister Jim was bewildered by the whole thing, but Mother couldn't have been happier that I was free. I confided the day after the divorce that Frank and I would be married. She said, "Well, of course. And you'll be moving to Iron River." I was twenty-six that winter, and in better health. The promise of Frank Bond's love was crowding out all the guilt and pain of the past, and my melodies, often silent during the bad years, sang in my head once again.

There were many, many letters from those years. I have them all, some stained with tears, others torn in anger, then patched back together to be re-read and cherished. They say over and over in a hundred different ways, "I Love You Truly." Despite our hidden relationship and the distance between us, Frank and I re-played the exciting games of our courtship. He had been my only love since I was fourteen. Our sin had caused us to lose years we could never recover. My greater sin lay in hurting a decent man who had worshipped me and married me in good faith, but had come to hate me in my fragile health and my unspoken dismissal of him as a man.

Edward Smith was also released from the prison of that marriage. Within a year he married Grace Norris, one of our old Janesville crowd, and they were soon parents of a boy.

And I began my Iron River adventure with Frank Bond.

Perhaps, finally, we could begin to forgive each other. And ourselves.

CHAPTER 12

DR. & MRS. FRANK BOND

Frank's father D.W. Bond closed his Johnstown practice and pharmacy while Frank was still studying at Rush Medical College in Chicago. D.W. was born in Virginia in 1828, left home at fifteen, and worked his way west as best he could, educating himself along the way. Like so many others who survived the hardships of the move west, he came out of it a master of many skills. He knew about metallurgy and geology and was an untrained but tough-minded engineer. He was a competent cellist, spoke pretty good German, and picked up other languages easily when he moved into the immigrant's world of Michigan's iron country. And yes, he was a "doctor." He attended "The Chicago Medical School," or so he said. It may have been Rush Medical, where he later sent Frank.

In Johnstown Center and Janesville he had been a trusted physician. Like so many medical men of his time, he was also a pharmacist, had owned the drugstore in Johnstown Center and opened one in Iron River soon as he had settled in. But it was no secret that D.W. Bond had a bad case of mining fever. Not for gold or silver. Those ores were out west, and he had traveled as far in that direction as he had ever wanted. In Great Lakes country the talk was of massive iron and copper deposits. Those ores, he told his friends, "were as good as gold."

I didn't know all this about D.W. Bond until Frank Bond and I were married and had moved to Iron River. Frank explained that D.W. had begun his explorations ten or more years before. Along with a partner by the name of MacKinnon, he was among the first to locate a major iron deposit in that northern wilderness. Within a few years Michigan's Upper Peninsula became for a time the largest iron-producing area in the United States. Immense fortunes were made and lost, but not by the Bonds, father or son.

I hardly knew D.W.'s wife Jane or Frank's sister Lily until I joined them in Iron River. Frank Bond was already well-established there. Remember, he had left Wisconsin for good in the fall of 1880, after he and I had fought so terribly. Frank had already joined his father's Iron River practice downtown on Genessee Street, with the customary drug store attached.

Living under the same roof with the Bond family for almost two years, I learned to tolerate the distant and difficult Jane Bond, and to adore Frank's fun-loving sister Lily. She taught school in the next village of Stambaugh, where she broke the hearts of dozens of miners and lumberjacks. She never married, and after Frank's death moved to St. Paul and never came back. Jane Bond had been D.W.'s childhood sweetheart in Virginia, and when he brought her west as his wife, he must have treated her like the hired girl. She was quiet to the point of rudeness, and she waited on D.W. with such servility that I chided Frank Bond he'd best not expect similar treatment. Frank Bond's death followed by just a few months that of his father's. D.W. had passed away earlier in 1895 with a paralytic stroke. His widow Jane Bond stayed on in Iron County and died, I think, in 1904.

It was June of 1889 when I joined my new husband Dr. Frank Bond in Iron River. I was no longer Carrie Jacobs-Smith. I was now Carrie Jacobs-Bond! How proud I was of that new name — even if I wasn't especially proud of our new home town. Back in 1926 I was asked to write an article for the *Ladies Home Journal* about my years in that dreadful place. Here's a part of what it said:

Our existence in the great pine forests was almost idyllic...Nature at its loveliest, most charming guise.

Carrie Jacobs-Smith-Bond! We didn't live in the woods, we lived right in Iron River itself, and it was a shabby, bad-smelling frontier mining town. The streets were muddy half the year and dusty the other half. Horse manure was a constant challenge to long skirts. Dogs fought with raccoons and pack rats over the garbage piled in most yards. We lived with Frank's parents for the first two years in a small flat above the drugstore run by Frank and D.W. There wasn't much room. Frederic was seven years old when we moved up north. He had to share the bedroom with us at first, until in desperation we moved him onto a cot in the parlor.

...we felt no need for many folks, for we had our great love.

Well, that was certainly true. I had to be madly in love with that man to live like we did those first years. But the many "folks" we didn't need? Ha! The elder Bonds knew everybody in town, from the wealthy Selden and MacKinnon families who founded the town and were D.W. Bond's mining partners, to the tough immigrant men who worked the iron mines and filled our little medical clinic and drugstore with the woes of their wives and children, not to mention their own. When Frank and D.W. weren't setting broken arms and legs, they were dispensing drugs and painkillers to keep the people (and the mines) of Iron River County functioning. Frank and I may not have had many real friends those first years, but there were often more "folks" than I could bear.

Sometimes I would drive with the doctor through the vast woods... While he tended the sick, I would linger in those great silences... interrupted by the murmuring of the wind in the trees.

My husband was a skilled and caring doctor — more so than his father, who had become careless and preoccupied with mining interests. But I should have told the *Journal* readers that after a few months with Frank Bond in Iron River, I was well into unofficial training as a nurse and druggist. More and more, I accompanied Frank on his calls to the nearby mining and lumber camps to help him deliver a baby, soothe a fevered child, set a broken bone, and yes — pronounce a death and file the certificate next day with the county clerk. You must understand that I did these things willingly and quite well. After all, I was no stranger to medical disciplines, not only because of Father's profession but because of the treatments and confinements I endured as a child.

Occasionally, on account of the density of the forest, the doctor and I would have to walk ten miles to some distant homesteader, and then I would go into the quiet woods and sit motionless while I thought out the verses of a song.

Carrie, how you do go on! Forgive me, Dear Reader, not only for hopeless exaggeration but some pretty awful writing! Dr. Bond and I never walked more than a mile or so to visit the sick. We had horses and a sturdy wagon. We drove that wagon plenty of times ten miles or more over narrow roads choked with mud in summer or drifted snow in the winter. If I ever had the chance to sit motionless in the woods while I waited for Dr. Bond, I don't remember it. I was usually too busy holding a newborn baby or emptying a slop jar or mixing a mustard plaster to think about music. But I must tell you — my music returned to me. The melodies *did* keep coming, wherever I was. Frank Bond, bless him, never failed to make me sit down and write them out. But I felt less urgency about it, and my dream of succeeding as a writer of songs was less persistent. I shall never gainsay that my years with Frank in Iron River were the happiest of my life. I could have lived and died there with him at my side and written my music for the church and for my piano students. My ambition burned low for a few years, but flared again in 1893, when we found ourselves in desperate need of money and I went to Chicago to sell my songs. When Frank died my ambition rejoined my music, and hasn't left me to this day.

CHAPTER 13

THE BOHEMIAN CLUB

The Depression year 1893 was a time of hardship for Frank and me, but less so than it was for the out-of-work miners and their families. Looking back it's hard to believe that any of us survived as well as we did. But that one bad year hasn't dented my memory of the years in Iron River as the happiest of my life. We had our cottage, our beloved son, and our friends. Both the doctors Bond, but especially my brave and darling Frank, simply worked harder than ever, helping those in desperate need of care. There were babies to be delivered, broken bones to be splinted, teeth to be pulled — yes, they became dentists by necessity, with nurse Carrie often standing by. It was a long year — more than a year, really, with no recovery in sight. It seemed that for every birth certificate we signed, there was a death to pronounce next day.

At first Frank wouldn't agree with my plan to go to Chicago to sell my songs. He was fond of the songs. It was Frank who was always after me to write them out in my poor scrawl of a hand. Of course, it was terribly naïve of me to think I could race down to Chicago, find a publisher, and come home with some badly-needed money in a week's time. But that's what I thought, and Frank finally agreed.

By then Chicago was no mystery to me. Ten years earlier I had spent difficult months there with Edward in our misbegotten attempt to train him in the tailor's trade. So I knew Chicago was big and dirty. It was years later that I read Lincoln Steffens' words, that Chicago was "first in violence, deepest in dirt; loud, lawless, unlovely, ill-smelling, irreverent, *new*." All too true, but if I'd heard them then, the only word I'd have embraced was "new." And I'd add "exciting." I got off the train giddy with hopes — a few dollars in my purse and absolutely no idea where or how to begin.

Uncle George was none to happy to see me. Mother had written him about the divorce, and after the standard lecture men felt they had to deliver about the "Sanctity of Marriage" he made room for me, and told me he was glad I'd gotten rid of that "good-for-nothing" husband. He had never met my Dr. Bond, but said any man would be an improvement. And how long did I plan to stay? His shop was on Wabash Avenue, with an attic room upstairs for me — good enough for my first Chicago adventure in publishing my music.

I was soon to learn that selling a song was a site more difficult that writing one. I had it in my head that if a newspaper would say something about one of my songs, publishers would come calling. Thus equipped with worldly wisdom I went to the office of the Chicago *Herald* and sent my card up to Mr. Scott, the editor. He couldn't have been nicer, as if having a shy, stammering woman call without introduction and fumble hand-written little songs from her handbag was an every day occurrence. He heard me out politely and then sent me downstairs to see a writer by the name of "Amber," who edited features for the *Herald*. "If you can interest her as you have me," he said, "she can do whatever she wants with your story."

In private life she was Mrs. Holden, but I could see why her *nom de plume* was Amber. She had the most beautiful eyes I'd ever seen — amber indeed, and they were filled that day with a kindness I have never forgotten. I soon found she was a favorite at the old Bohemian Club — its members mostly writers and artists — a gathering to which distinguished guests felt honored to attend. (Amber, I later found, was called the Queen of Bohemia.) I spent the afternoon with her, and she took me to Thompson's restaurant for dinner. We talked and talked, and she ended up convincing me I should play some of my little songs that very night at the Bohemian Club.

Up through a darkened building on a side street near the *Herald* office we climbed three flights and entered a spooky candle-lit room, with a beer keg and a coffee urn side-by-side on a long table. The Bohemian Club!

Well! Eugene Field was there and recited some of his verses. Two years later he'd be gone but we remember him yet, and I've thought about that night every time I've read his "Wynken, Blyknen and Nod" to my grandchildren. Dear Opie Read charmed me instantly. Years later, when I misspelled his name as "Reed" in *Roads of Melody,* he wrote me with a line I'll bet he'd used a thousand times: "Mrs. Bond, can't you *Read?"* He was a delight. My, but Chicago was just brimming with talent in those days. George Ade was a Bohemian, soon enough a famous playwright, and author of his delightful *Fables.* Few people remember Ben King any more but he was the cock-of-the-walk that night, reciting some verses that he'd written that very day (he said) — very funny and just a bit naughty. John Vance Cheney was there, and to be honest I've never cared much for his poetry, but I must say he was the most polite and courtly of all the famous and soon-famous people I met that night.

The most famous-to-be was Pete Dunne. He was the boy wonder of the Chicago newspaper crowd — had been city editor of the *Post* before he was twenty, and in those Gay-90s days he was the talk-of-the town with his "Mister Dooley" stories. He was the proper and perfect gentleman, and he refused to recite any of his latest stories in the Irish brogue that he used for Mister Dooley. Before long he'd be the most widely-read columnist in America, after his hilarious column about Teddy Roosevelt in Cuba (very sarcastic, really) was picked up all over the country. He left for New York and became the editor for several big magazines, but he kept up his stories from Mr. Dooley's Southside Chicago saloon for many years. It seemed like every newspaper printed them every Sunday. He didn't have much to say to me that night, and I thought him a bit of a stuffed-shirt. His full name was Peter Finley Dunne but he changed it to Finley Peter Dunne because he thought it sounded better, I guess. I had to laugh, a man insisting on a third name — like William *Randolph* Hearst. We "new" women were doing it, but for us it was a way to keep part of our own names — Margaret Culkin Banning, Elizabeth Cady Stanton, Carrie Jacobs Bond.

And Grace Duffie Boylan. She was a Bohemian, like Amber another woman in that man's world of Chicago newspapers. How I admired them! Dear Amber passed on just a few years later, but Grace became a friend for life. Her books for children would soon bring her fame and fortune, but it was her mysterious pamphlet *Thy Son Liveth* in 1918 that would help me endure my greatest sorrow, the death of my son Frederic.

It was after midnight when Amber announced she had "brought her friend Carrie," who might be coaxed into playing some of her new songs. I was awfully nervous and the piano was horribly out of tune, but I played for about half-an-hour, and everyone was most kind. I didn't realize until after I finished that Ethelbert Nevin had come in while I was playing. He was very encouraging to me. Of course, he was a famous classical musician who had studied in Europe, but he said he adored the simplicity of my songs, and had tried to compose more "for the people" himself. I have a secret little thought that my songs might just have inspired him that way. He was the composer of many lovely and difficult pieces for the piano, but just a few years on, 1898 I think, he came out with *The Rosary* — so beautiful, so simple. Everybody sang it then and sing it to this day. He especially liked my *Just A-Wearyin' for You.* I admitted that the words weren't mine, but a poem by a Mr. Frank Stanton that I had run across. He jotted down the name. I like to think his sweet song *Mighty Lak' a Rose* came from of our chat, because it used another Frank Stanton poem. It swept the country in 1901. That same year we finally published my little song, and it later became almost as popular as his. Mr. Nevin died that year. I think it was of consumption. He was thirty-eight years old. It crosses my mind as I write this that just a few years ago the world lost another great composer at age thirty-eight — George Gershwin. Who knows what beautiful music went to the grave with those two men.

I still hold the joy of that glorious night at the Bohemian Club as the height of my Chicago memories. Everyone was so kind. Next morning I went right to Amber's office to thank her again. She said, "Now what do you want to do next, Carrie?" And of course I said I want to meet with a publisher — someone who will see there's money to be made with my songs. Right away she thought of a Mr. Brigham, head of a Chicago firm I'd heard of. She made an appointment for me, and that very day I was at the piano in their office doing three or four of my little songs. Mr. Brigham was very cordial. "I'm sure you'll be able to sell those songs, Mrs. Bond," he said, "But what we're looking for right now are children's songs. Do you have any of those?"

I didn't. But nervy me, I said of course I did, and went back to my room — no piano of course — and wrote two new songs, words and music. One was called *Is My Dolly Dead?*

I dropped Dolly, broke her head
Someone told me Dolly's dead,
Tell me, Dolly, is it true
I can no more play with you?

Mr. Brigham liked it. He said they'd publish it, and he fished out some papers offering me a royalty agreement. I was so excited I don't think I even read them. There was a nice "advance" — $35.00 I think. Some years later Bond & Son took back the copyright, but those were the first real dollars earned by my songs. I think I left copies of my other songs on the piano, and I heard not another word from Mr. Bingham. But I was thrilled, and thrilled again when I took the news of the Dolly song to Amber. She said, "We're going right now to see my friend Teresa Vaughn. She's here in Chicago with the show *Fourteen-Ninety-Two.*" And Miss Vaughn "interpolated" the song as her encore the next evening!

Next day Amber and I went to the Fair and rode the Ferris Wheel. And I took the afternoon train back to Iron River with Mr. Brigham's cheque tucked in my purse, convinced I'd made a great mistake waiting to publish my songs for so long. It was easy. Little did I know. I was still a babe in the woods.

CHAPTER 14

THE MANSFIELD

Twenty-seven men died on May 15, 1893 when the Michigamme River flooded the main shaft of the Mansfield Mine near Iron River. The poor souls must have been surprised at their moment of death to be buried by water, rather than by fearful tons of falling rock that ended lives below ground with grim regularity. Iron County people were used to it. Miners would be trapped, cut off, sometimes to die down there. Many's the time I held a weeping child to my breast as we waited through the night to learn of Daddy's fate. Once it was a little girl who'd been taking piano lessons from me, another time a sickly boy whose sad eyes and runny nose I remembered from his anxious visits to Dr. Bond's infirmary. On lucky days their tears, along with those of wives and mothers, turned quickly into choking cheers as their blackened menfolk reached sunlight and safety. But there were dark times, when the wailing of a new-made widow echoed off the hills, and the bloody remnants of her crushed beloved were hoisted to the surface.

But the Mansfield disaster was different.

Dear God, it was awful. Workmen in the yard that morning near the Mansfield headframe say they heard an unearthly roar — an alien thunder that they knew was not the customary muffle of blasting powder below. The swollen Michigamme had broken through a hundred feet down. They watched in horror as the silted water spurted up the shaft in seconds, spilling over the ground at their feet. They knew their comrades below were already drowning as the waters sought out the horizontal drifts where the doomed men were at work.

Men were killed or injured on an almost daily basis in Iron County. Until the Depression hit us in 1893, the mines and the lumber mills were running full out. The Chicago and Northwestern Railroad had cut across the Upper Peninsula in 1885, and Iron County prospered. The ore trains traveled seventy-five miles west over to Ironwood, near the Lake, and loaded boats bound for foundries in Illinois and Ohio. Logs of the massive white pine that still carpeted the Upper Peninsula traveled east, to be dumped into the Menominee River and floated down Lake Michigan to Milwaukee and Chicago. I often thought as I walked the streets of Chicago a few years later, that the timbers and the cast iron in its buildings had come down from our dismal county.

Iron mines and white pines! Leave it to me to find the rhymes around me. This one sounded romantic, but I knew better. The mines and the pines were deadly enemies to the men who worked them, most of whom were just off the boat from a dozen different countries in Europe. They had little education and couldn't speak English. To the owners they were just a step above indentured servants. Injury and death were to be expected. If a man didn't lose a leg to a runaway ore cart or an arm to a whirling saw blade, he plunged into lifelong paralysis or sudden death while topping a 100-foot white pine.

The lumberjacks at least were working in the open air. Down in the damp and darkness of his 12-hour day, the iron miner slaved under conditions that would not be tolerated today. The Union Movement was far in the future. (That great friend of today's miners, John L. Lewis, was a 13-year-old boy growing up in Iowa when the Mansfield flooded.)

Those men died in utter darkness.

Did you ever go down into a mine? I did a time or two, with Dr. Bond. Compared to a mine's darkness, a moonless night is bright and cheery. The acetylene or electric lamps you see now on their helmets were undreamed of then. Miners worked by candlelight, and in most of the mines were forced to buy the candles from the owner's commissary! Sometimes to save money, three or four of them would work by the light of just one candle. Dr. Frank Bond did away with that in the Mansfield and the other Bond mines. I'm sorry to say he did so over the objections of his father. D.W. Bond went along with the thinking of most owners. "That's just the way it's done, Frank. These fellows don't know any better. They're lucky to have the work and they know it."

Frank and D.W. Bond rushed to the Mansfield. I went with them — drove the buggy while they shouted at each other about what they should have brought along. We didn't yet know how bad it was — just that some men were trapped. When we reached the mine we saw they needed nothing, that there was nothing anyone could do, not even retrieve the bodies. We came upon one lucky miner named Johnson who was lying in a daze a few yards away. He'd been caught at just the right moment as the water geysered up the shaft. It had picked him up and deposited him gently near the headframe. Dr. Bond told me to give him a whisky and send him home.

It was obvious that the others in the gathering crowd needed neither whisky nor medicine. They needed hope, where there was none. I moved through the crowd trying to calm the wives and children with what we all knew were lies. If their man was down there, he was already dead.

A screeching Croatian woman clawed her way to confront D.W. Bond and spat in his face. She and a few others began chanting a chorus of shame — that it was his fault, that he knew the mine was unsafe, that he knew the Michigamme was dangerously high. He stood there in silence, tears wetting his face. I'm certain he realized there was truth in their cries. As a physician he could not have been more kind and dedicated. In his other role as a mine-owner and operator, he seemed untroubled by the accepted doctrine of the day: Labor existed to serve Capital. Capital, in turn, uplifted the Laborer. Of course there would be accidents and hardship, but they were a necessary part of the March of Progress.

Not long after the Mansfield tragedy, a young congressman from Nebraska, William Jennings Bryan, gave a speech over in Superior. Frank and I, Dr. D.W., Mr. and Mrs. Selden and several others took the train there to hear him. I remember his voice was like a trumpet, and he gave a fiery speech about the duties of Capital to working people. Who knew then he would be nominated for president three times — "The Great Commoner" to millions of Americans?

After the speech one of the Iron River owners said, "That man is little better than a dangerous anarchist!" D.W., even Frank, may have agreed, but I was angry enough to say, "After all we've seen, isn't it time someone spoke up for the men down there?" We met Mr. Bryan briefly after the speech. I remember thinking the hand I shook belonged to a *man.* I always believed in him.

Dr. D.W. Bond died a year or so later of a stroke or a seizure of some kind. In our grief his son and I wondered if this good man's struggle between the compassion of a physician and the hardness of business-as-usual finally broke his spirit.

It was days before the swollen Michigamme retreated enough to allow crews of heartbroken men to enter the horror below, and bring out the bodies of their fathers and sons and brothers. When the Bonds were finally called upon to examine and identify them as best they could, it was unbearable. The corpses were blanched and bloated. Some had been further desecrated by rats that had survived the flood in slanted drifts and found life for themselves amongst the dead.

The names of the martyrs could have been read from the list of newly-naturalized United States citizens published every six months in the Iron County *Reporter* — proud names, some still unpronounceable, others, like the charmed Mr. Johnson, revised by impatient immigration officials at their point of entry. Hordes of newcomers from all over Europe —Scots, Germans, Finns, Croatians, Irish, Norwegians — came to the woods and the mines in hopes of sharing their bounty. A handful of them got rich in Iron County and left to build handsome homes in Milwaukee and Minneapolis. A few others, like our friends the MacKinnons and the Seldens, kept their money where they had made it. They stayed on in Iron County and helped to civilize that hard, unforgiving country. But most ended their lives in city shacks or on tiny farms, fighting through the merciless winters, probably dreaming of locating just one more outcropping of hematite.

The Mansfield Mine was the biggest producer in the area, close by Iron River. Both my husband and my father-in-law had heavy investments in the Mansfield, and in the Paint and Calipurnia mines nearby. They told me very little about these things, but it was rumored that D.W. Bond owned 51 per cent of the Mansfield. As early as 1880 he and his partner "Mac" MacKinnon had located the Crystal Falls mine, one of the earliest discoveries. Long before Frank Bond and I were married and I moved north with him, I became aware it was not the promise of a good medical practice that had brought him and his father to Iron County. It was the mines. They came to that wilderness to make money.

Not that they neglected the practice of medicine. Both, Frank especially, were revered for their services to the county people. When the district fell on bad times — and it did go down hard in the Depression of 1893, the Bonds went down with the town folk. But they stayed on. They sold their drugstore and devoted themselves to medical practice, more desperately needed now than ever before. I went with both of them on countless emergencies, summer and winter. One day it would be a breech birth, the next a shattered spine. I held a three-year-old girl in my arms as diphtheria strangled the life out of her. In those harsh days Dr. Bond often took payment in a side of bacon or a cord of firewood. Or no payment at all.

Frank Bond should not have died. He was thirty-seven years old. No one was more capable, tough, *alive* than he. For years I have replayed over and over the sequence that led to his death. Usually, when Dr. Bond was summoned to treat to a patient on one of Iron River's bitter nights, the errand was urgent. He would rush to hitch up the wagon or sometimes just throw a saddle over one of our three horses and be on his way. On that fateful November evening in 1895, the air was warm and clear. Yesterday's three-inch flurry was melting down just right for snowballing. My sweet man for once was in no hurry, and he stopped over by Genessee Street to join a neighborhood snowball fight. Running and shouting with the boys and girls, he fell hard against a jutting stone. He got right up, the children said later, and assured them he was fine, that he hadn't hit his head, just "his tummy."

Five days later he died of a ruptured spleen.

CHAPTER 15

HARD TIMES

I woke up this morning thinking about death. You say, "Of course, we all do at times." Well, I don't and never have. I'm 83 years old. Since I was a child I have spent weeks on end in hospitals and sanitariums, and have cheated death twice — that I know of. I have witnessed the death of my parents, my husbands, my son and most of my friends. Two years ago my beloved May Robson left this earth. Each death shattered me, but each death then challenged me to go on with my own life. I have never contemplated my own death. Until this morning.

I am an old woman. I looked at myself in the mirror and viewed what the friendly writers call "my halo of snow-white hair." I saw only grim gray that once was rich and black. I saw a woman who struggles each day to keep straight the shoulders and spine her father demanded of her ages ago. I stood in the redwood parlor of my Pinehurst home with the sun pouring in on a fall morning, and for the first time in memory heard no new melody to glorify the moment. If that seems trivial you must understand that to me, whose river of melody has flowed nearly unchecked since childhood, it was a most profound sign.

That's when I determined I must write again about my life. And my death. It's coming soon. I have stipulated in no uncertain terms with Rose Ives and Jaime that none of what you're reading be published until well after I'm gone.

I have an appointment with Dr. Marshall this afternoon. He saw me through my long hospital stay last year — five months in Wilshire House — a rest home, really. He is a physician so much to my liking — kind and thoughtful and willing to listen. So many of those I saw after Frank Bond's death treated me as just another emotionally troubled female. In those days the medical men dismissed half of the complaints of women as "hysteria," when in truth they had little understanding of a women's life.

"I had been an invalid for years," I wrote in *Roads of Melody*, "and I was no longer young." I don't know why on earth I used the word "invalid" to describe my condition after Frank's death. I shouldn't have. I think of an invalid as a person who wants never to get well, get back to work, stay in the world. I always did. My years with Frank Bond in Iron River were not only the happiest of my life, they were the healthiest. Of course I was still plagued, as I am to this day, by the damages of the crippling accident in my childhood. Through the years I often explained that my frequent hospitalizations were due to "inflammatory rheumatism," and there's no denying I've spent many months in hospitals and sanitariums. Dr. Marshall thinks I may also have had rheumatic fever, brought on by a bout with scarlet fever when I was four. He says for certain I have never suffered from rheumatoid arthritis or I wouldn't even be alive today, much less able to live as actively as I do.

Yet I feel I must clear the air about my references in *Roads of Melody* to my poor health.

There is a moment of birth and there is a moment of death. We are suddenly here and then, just as suddenly, not. Somehow we are always surprised by death. It comes for most of us in such ordinary moments. Wouldn't we all like to die in that "Blaze of Glory" they talk about? Dying in bed of pneumonia or after a fall on the porch steps seems such a failure. But my dear dead Avery Harris used to say "Carrie, to live is to fail. Every one of us fails, because every one of us dies."

His own life was marked by earthly failure followed by sweet success, ended, as he said, by our ultimate failure — death.

I don't want to believe Frank Bond's death was failure. He was still working, learning, *doing*, the day he died in that stupid accident. Sudden death confounds us utterly, doesn't it? He wasn't ready, couldn't prepare. Why Frank? Why then? I refuse to believe in predestination or the hand of the Divine. Frank's goodness and mercies far outweighed his sins, such as they were. God had nothing to do with the death of my Beloved.

This old woman knows for sure that she would never have been the success the world thinks she is if Frank Bond had not died that December day in 1895. I was thirty-three years old, a settled woman with a fourteen-year-old son and a husband who was kind and respected and, even after our run of bad luck in the early '90s, on his way to better things. Instead, he was buried by his devoted lodge brothers on another December day four days later — heartbreakingly one of the last of Indian Summer, the snowstorm that took his life having melted away.

The brothers that buried him came to me a week later with a cheque for $3,900 — the proceeds from a life insurance policy carried by their lodge. Frank had never mentioned it. I knew he and D.W. had scorned the fast-growing commercial insurance companies of that day — some scandal-ridden. But here were real dollars — a last hug and kiss from that good man.

By the time I paid our debts and closed our mortgaged home, I had less than $2000 left, a son to care for, and no skills that I could use to earn a living. I said goodbye to our Iron River friends, and returned to Janesville with a broken heart and a body so pain-ridden that I could barely raise it mornings from the bed.

There was nothing for me in Janesville but loneliness and painful memories. Edward Smith had remarried — one of the Norris girls from Johnstown Center by the name of Grace. They had a little boy already five years old. That meant my Frederic had, legally at least, a half-brother whom he had never met. (Never would, by the way.) I stayed with friends just long enough to realize I had to leave, but with time to write two songs in memory of my dear Frank Bond. My big "hit," *I Love You Truly* was truly written for Frank, but you may wonder why, on the sheet music it is dedicated to A.B.H.[*] My other song for Frank, published in my *Book of Seven Songs* in 1901 was *Shadows.* I considered it the better of the two songs, and longed to share it with the world. But it never caught on.

I know you're way off yonder, but still you seem with me
And through the evening shadows your form I almost see,
I almost hear you whisper these words, "I love but you,"
And soon we'll be united, sweetheart, be brave, be true.

Though my health was poor, I was now more confident than ever in my ability to write songs and sell them. I took the balance of the insurance money and put it out at interest, and left for Chicago.

I had some furniture from Iron River and some from Janesville. I had it all moved into a rented house near Chicago's College of Physicians and Surgeons. I was determined to rent out a couple of rooms to provide some income, and felt sure medical students would be desirable tenants. Most were wonderful young men, some as poor as I was. In those grim Chicago years I was fast learning that there's only one way to really know people, and that is to be as poor as they are. There are always plenty of friends on a sunny day.

A story still follows me around that I ran a boarding house in those early Chicago days. Not so, just a rooming house, but wouldn't you know? Before long I was offering those hard-working young fellows snacks, then breakfast, then packing a lunch for them. Before a year was out my savings were nearly gone, and Frederic and I moved to a smaller place on 42 East 31st Street. Even there the rent of $15 a month was too high. Still, it offered three spacious rooms on the second floor, and had its own bathroom. There was a restaurant on the ground floor run by a Miss McGraw, who in no time proved a fast friend. I was earning a few dollars hand-painting china — a vogue in the 1890's. But more dollars were going out than coming in, and winter was ahead — a Chicago winter. We couldn't afford wood and coal to heat the whole house, so Frederic and I closed off the back room.

Lots of people in Chicago that winter were far worse off than we were. One afternoon a half-frozen young fellow knocked on the door and said he would shovel the sidewalk. He wanted ten cents. Even that was more than I could easily pay, but he was so distressed and

---

* *Avery Bancroft Harris*

pathetically cold that I invited him in for a cup of hot tea. He sat by our fire rubbing his frozen hands, and I offered him some bread and jam. He surprised me with, "Thank you, Mrs. Bond."

"How in the world do you know my name," I asked him.

"I can't blame you for not recognizing me, Mrs. Bond. I rented a room from you last year when I was at the medical college. My name is Avery Harris."

I did remember him, though he had roomed with us for only a month or so. "What in the world has happened to you, dear boy?" I couldn't believe he had come down in the world like this in so short a time.

"Mrs. Bond," he said, "you told us your father and your late husband were physicians, so I hope you'll understand. I became an addict. I became addicted to cocaine."

I recalled that Frank and D.W. Bond had just begun to try this new discovery as an anesthetic. Doctors in Europe were hailing it as a fantastic boon, a pain-killer of unbelievable power. But addicted? "We were told the drug was totally benign," he said, "a godsend in surgery and treatment of pain. I wasn't the only one trapped. Two others that I know of also left training. God knows where they are."

I could not send Avery Harris away into the dreadful cold. "Where are you going to sleep tonight?"

"I don't know," he said

"Well, it's settled. You'll stay here. I have a back room with no heat but plenty of blankets. You'll sleep there."

He stayed for three months. Next day, warm, washed, dressed in some decent clothes I'd kept of Frank Bond's, he surprised me again. He noticed on the piano some of my sorry efforts at writing down music. I may have had a good hand at watercolors and china painting, but my musical manuscripts were (and still are) an awkward mess.

"Mrs. Bond," he said, "I can do that for you. I studied violin and I coached a college glee club for two years. I do a pretty good manuscript."

His manuscripts were not just good, they were perfect. You have no idea how they helped me in the coming years to deal with printers and performers, who blanched at my poor handiwork.

Avery Harris lived in that back room of ours for three months. He found odd jobs, for a while even assisting in the labs at the college. I have no idea how he dealt with his addiction. He must have suffered terribly, but I know he eventually won over it. His reason for leaving us is further testament to his good heart. He came home one evening in March, an evening of cold and snow as only March in Chicago can bring.

"Carrie, Freddie," he said, "Come out here right away." We pulled on galoshes and overcoats, and Avery led us into an alley several blocks away, where a poor man and his wife and three children had been dispossessed. They and their few belongings had been set out into the snow. We brought them to the house. "They'll take my room," Avery said, "the back room. I was going to leave anyway." I couldn't argue. The little family — the Bidermans — had nowhere else to go.

They stayed for many months. This part of the story has two happy endings. Another, not so happy, is that not long after they came and Avery Harris left, I had a severe attack of what the doctors were then calling inflammatory rheumatism. I could literally not move from my bed. That little Biderman family took care of me, with Frederic's help, until I was back on my feet. Then Mr. Biderman finally got a job as a drayman, and they were able to get back into a place of their own.

I didn't hear from Avery Harris for several years. It was after my first few song successes, and Frederic and I had established The Bond Shop and were beginning to do well in the publishing business. Avery was back in Chicago applying for a position as choir director of the beautiful Presbyterian Church on Michigan Avenue, just rebuilt after its awful 1900 fire. He got the job. He had conquered his addiction.

Avery and I began a loving relationship that lasted for a number of years. Let me explain what that expression means to me. I may have invented it.

I was widowed at the age of thirty-three. My marriage to Dr. Bond brought me every happiness a marriage can bring. My friends, my mother, even Frederic wondered why I never married again. I was attractive enough, I suppose, and after the hard Chicago years had become a woman of means. But I was past forty before the money worries were behind me. I relished every minute in the exciting whirl of success those next Chicago years brought me. I lived in a fever of creativity. I had learned how to market the songs that flooded my brain, and how to bask in the acclaim they brought me. Profits for Bond &

Son neared the embarrassing. Parties and performances crowded my evenings. I didn't need or a want a man. I wanted friends.

Not long after Frank Bond died and the hard years began, I realized my years on earth had led me to a simple truth: *friendship is everything.* Friends were all I would need and all I would seek for the rest of my life. No one would ever replace Frank Bond. But others — men and women — could love me and be loved in return. *Friends.* Some friendships would be casual, others profound. With a close friend, my deepest personal needs would be shared and met. I knew I couldn't live without others, but those others, I would insist, would always be of my choosing.

My loving relationship with a young Avery Harris, as you have seen, began with pity. It changed gradually to real affection as we worked together with music. We found in one another an unspoken sense of comfort and understanding, and best of all, a playfulness I could never have imagined with a man. We saw each other often during the Chicago years. Even after he married in 1905 our relationship continued discreetly, until the Harrises moved to Europe around 1909.

CHAPTER 16

ELBERT HUBBARD

I sat down at my desk last May 7th planning to tell the story of my first and only effort to make a phonograph record years ago. As usual I turned on the radio first and I think I must have shouted for joy when I heard the news that the war in Europe was over — "V-E Day," they were calling it. The Germans had surrendered and Hitler was dead. An hour later Jaime came in with the newspapers and we sat on the porch with our coffee devouring the details. Almost by accident an item on an inside page caught my eye. May 7th was also the 30th anniversary of the sinking of the *Lusitania*! If you remember that dreadful day in 1915, you'll share my wave of sorrow — so many dead, helpless, so close to shore. We were still haunted by the death of the *Titanic* three years before, but this was somehow even more ghastly. The *Titanic's* deadly iceberg seemed somehow innocent compared to the German torpedo that left over a thousand dead, almost two hundred of them Americans. It began the national fury that drove us two years later into the awful war in Europe.

I found myself pouring out a flood of memories to Jaime, and asked her to remind me to take notes I'd want to use. Think of it. The Germans sank the *Lusitania* in 1915. Twenty-five years later they had conquered most of Europe. Now, five years after that, they're beaten again and Europe is a shambles. How could a scant thirty years produce such killing and horror?

Thoughts of two men from those times clicked in together — men whose memory I still admire: Elbert Hubbard and William Jennings Bryan. I shall never forget meeting Mr. Bryan — I think in 1894 —when he spoke about the plight of the working men in the mining country up north. Both Frank and I were overwhelmed by his compassion and his very presence. Then two years later, with Frank gone, Frederic and I silently cheered Mr. Bryan from our little flat in Chicago when the convention right there at Coliseum nominated him for president in 1896. He was just 36 years old that summer, when he made his famous "cross of gold" speech. Two more times he tried for the White House — and lost. Jaime was still in school in 1925, and she didn't remember a thing about poor Mr. Bryan's humiliation at the "monkey" trial in Tennessee, though it was in all the papers for weeks. The poor man passed away back there a few days later. Most people made fun of him — still do, if they remember him at all. But some of us don't forget that Mr. Bryan was the only man in Washington who stood up against the war fever, and that he was noble enough to quit his job as Secretary of State, after he predicted President Wilson was getting us into a war we ought to stay out of.

My special agony about the *Lusitania* was the dreadful news that my dear friend Elbert Hubbard and his wife had perished — on their way to Germany, he told the newspapers, to see if he could meet with Kaiser Wilhelm himself. By then Elbert had traveled the world, talking to people in every walk of life and publishing them in his *Little Journeys* books. Jaime and I actually found ourselves laughing after I showed her some pictures of both Hubbard and Bryan and she pointed out they were look-alikes. I'd never thought of it, but yes — both were very handsome men with slowly receding hairlines, offset by long flowing locks in back. Both affected fashionable clothing — coats and cravats not the stuff of lesser men. I had known Mr. Bryan only casually, but my feelings for Elbert Hubbard ran deep. He was my inspiration. He challenged me to start Bond & Son and publish my own songs. He told me to be proud, not ashamed, to publish my own work. It wasn't vanity, he said, it was good business. He had done it himself.

Much was written about their last days on that doomed ship, and thinking about this 30th anniversary led me back to my Hubbard books — and to memories of the man himself, and the doors he opened for me when I was sunk in Chicago poverty so many years ago. Jaime and I decided the story of my phonograph records could wait, and that 7th day of May would be a good time to go back to my first meeting with that extraordinary man and tell you how he entered my life and changed it forever. Let me begin (I just looked these up) with two of my favorite quotations from "Fra Albertus" as he was sometimes called. This first one is now an everyday quip, but he said it first: "Life is just one damned thing after another." (I can just hear him!) The other one defined his life — and his death: "Don't take life too seriously. You'll never get out of it alive."

You know how in the Chicago days I imposed on friends to sponsor little recitals, usually for ten dollars. One such, in 1901, was held at the new Art Institute. Afterwards, a lovely auburn-haired women with the kindest eyes I ever saw, Mrs. Henry Howe, came up to me. She was from Iowa, she said, and the President of something called the 20th Century Club in Marshalltown. She invited me to come there and sing. They would pay all my expenses. I went, and it was a happy occasion. Through her efforts I then sang in almost every important town in the state of Iowa.

After a recital in Bloomfield I was taken to hear a lecture downtown by Elbert Hubbard. I knew next-to-nothing about his Roycroft Shop, just then getting started, but I had seen his magazine *The Philistine*, and thought he was a very unkind man. He said some things I thought quite rude. Then I heard him speak, and Oh! I changed my mind in a hurry. I'd never heard a more interesting talk in my entire life.

I cranked up my courage and shook hands with him and was bowled over when he said, "Ha! I know all about you, Mrs. Bond, through our mutual friend Grace Boylan. I know that *Auf Wiedersehn* song you two put together, and a couple of your other songs," he said. "I think they are lovely. Would you have time to see me in the next two days?" Would I!

We met the next day and without any preliminaries he asked, "What is it you want, Mrs. Bond? What are you looking for?" I stammered that I wanted to go to New York, where, I said, "the greatest opportunities for original things can be found." He told me months later, after we'd become close, that he had stifled a laugh at that. He knew better. And by then I was following his creed that you don't wait, you make your own opportunities. For both of us that meant becoming our own publisher — running our own business. I saw this in action on my first visit to his Roycroft Shop in East Aurora, New York. He invited me to begin little recitals there that grew into full concerts and continued right up to the month before his fateful trip. Following my first shaky recital, he wrote this in the *Philistine*:

> Here is a woman who writes poems, sets them to music, and sings them in a manner that reveals the very acme of art, tunes that sing themselves. But in some way they search out the corners of your soul.

I spent a week in East Aurora that first time, and then I watched Roycroft grow over the years into the center for art and publishing for which it's still remembered. As soon as I got back to 42 East 31st Street, I vowed to name our place "The Bond Shop" and go into the publishing business. Frederic thought it a wonderful idea, even better when I said our company's name would be Carrie Jacobs-Bond & Son, Inc.

For years, whenever I went East, I'd stop in East Aurora, and a recital was always welcomed. All the artists and helpers were invited into the beautiful music room, next to the old gymnasium where I had done my first concert. After Elbert's death, his son Elbert Jr., "Bert," took over, and did a wonderful job, until the Depression, I suppose, forced him to finally shut down in 1938. A few months after Elbert senior died, a beautiful bound book arrived from Roycroft, containing a tribute to me that was found among his things. Forgive me if I quote just a bit of it:

> Carrie Jacobs-Bond was along Roycroft way, and as usual, she sang for us. We quit work and gathered in the music room. Time has tempered her, she has cashed in all her experiences so today, all her actions are regal, gracious, chartered with honesty, flavored with success. One of her songs was *A Perfect Day*, more widely sold than any piece of music since Gilbert & Sullivan

> launched "Pinafore." It has passed the five million mark and has brought its composer thousands and thousands of dollars. Not bad for a lone, lorn widow.

I don't know just when he wrote that — maybe in 1914. People said by then he and the Roycrofters had changed forever how books are brought out. No more dark, stodgy bindings. The Roycrofters gave us design and color and fine paper. At Roycroft the books were handmade, but their ideas inspired the old-line publishers to liven things up.

I came to understand Elbert Hubbard as a writer, too. His magazine *The Philistine* I think set the stage for a lot of others to come. He hated superstition and narrow-minded traditions. I've heard it said he was a Rosicrucian. I've never been sure just what that means, but I like to think it had to do with his way of doubting our sacred cows, and his sense of fairness to all — not to mention his wonderful disposition.

How I loved that man. We treated one another with respect but with real affection. He was a hugger and a kisser. In private moments together he'd tease me with song titles of the day like *I Love My Wife, but Oh You Kid,* or he'd change the George Cohan song to *Carrie's a Grand Old Name.* I suppose I had a crush on him, but I was careful not to show it. Frederic asked me more than once if I was in love with Elbert Hubbard. I always said, "Every woman falls in love with that man, Frederic, but not just for his good looks and his charm. He makes us believe in ourselves. He's the most hopeful person I've ever met. And beside that, he's funny." Did our friendship go beyond that? I shall end these memories of Elbert Hubbard, Dear Reader, leaving you to wonder.

After that first visit to the Roycrofters, I took the long train ride to New York City. You won't believe how naïve I was — thinking the publishers would just jump at the chance to publish my little songs. I found out quickly that they wanted people who could write incidental music, or songs that could be interpolated in operas and musicals. And I found out that many of those Tin Pan Alley fellows wanted something else from this widow lady before they'd listen to her songs. Well, I couldn't do the one and wouldn't do the other, so my visits to their offices were brief and depressing.

I did hear from one of them that Della Fox was rehearsing a new comic opera, and that she was very kind and would probably see me.

So again I summoned my courage and marched into the theater where they were rehearsing. It was dark, and the first thing I saw was the light of a cigarette. Imagine my shock when I realized it was held by Miss Fox herself. Until that time I had never known a woman who smoked. (My, how that has changed!) I don't suppose anyone remembers her today, but people just loved her. She was naturally childlike, on and off stage. That's why I was so shocked to see her smoking a cigarette. Girls everywhere imitated her cute Della-Fox curl. I introduced myself in a very timid way, trying to handle my surprise that I was really talking to her while she was smoking!

She was just charming. "What kind of songs do you write?" I must have said they were simple and homey, and recited a few lines from *Where to Build Your Castle*, because it was the first one that came to my mind. "Well," she said, "that's not a song I would sing, but I have a lady in the company who could do it beautifully, and I'll get her to sing it." And she did. I'm ashamed that in my old book I said I didn't remember the name of the opera. (Carrie Jacobs-Bond! You could have looked it up!) It was *The Little Host*, her biggest hit. She toured in it for over a year. In that day they said she was the highest paid performer on the American variety stage.

Nothing more came of my first New York visit. With my ticket, still courtesy of Elbert Hubbard, I took the first train back to Chicago. And back to hard times.

CHAPTER 17

THE DREISER BROTHERS

One bitter-cold morning soon after I had moved to Chicago, I stopped by Amber Holden's office at the *Herald* to chat and warm up a bit. I had hardly taken off my coat when a string-bean young fellow pushed in behind me. My dear light-hearted Amber instantly became stern Mrs. Holden. She introduced the man, quite coldly I thought, as Theodore Dreiser, a reporter at the Chicago *Globe.* I could see he was irritated to find me there — an intruder into what was clearly his inept pursuit of Amber's affections, a pursuit just as clearly unwelcome on her part. Conversation floundered, and I recall almost nothing from the encounter. Nor could he, when we met briefly at a social gathering many years later here in Los Angeles, where he had lived until his death last year.

I hadn't realized on that Chicago afternoon that this Dreiser fellow was the younger brother of Paul Dresser, the famous songwriter whom I simply adored. I had broken into tears when I first played through his ballad *Just Tell Them That You Saw Me,* published I think in 1894. It tells the story of a young woman from a small town who comes to the City determined to make a success of her life. Instead she becomes, we believe, a "fallen" woman. In that day there were dozens of songs on that subject, most of them trash, marketed by self-important men sniggering through songs like *In the Heart of the City That Has No Heart* or *She is More to be Pitied Than Censured.* Paul Dresser had earlier written his share of sentimental potboilers, but this song was different. It was set to a melody that haunted the ear, the kind of melody I could write, the kind I *did* write — clear and logical, its harmonies sweet and direct. The words, I was sure, came from some deep well in his own heart — a well of sadness and regret.

In the song a gentleman meets a woman on the streets of the City. They had grown up together in the distant village: She pleads:

> *"Just tell them that you saw me,"*
> *She said, "They'll know the rest.*
> *Just tell them I was looking well, you know.*
> *Just whisper if you get a chance, to Mother dear and say,*
> *I love her as I did long, long ago."*

Some say that songwriters should never admit to writing songs about their own lives. It's never bothered me. I have never made it a secret that I composed *Shadows* and *I Love You Truly* in my grief over the death of Dr. Bond. *The End of a Perfect Day* literally flowed from me in celebration of a golden day spent with dear friends.

I was able to ask Paul Dresser about it. As you'll see, we had become close friends. I made it specific. "Who was the woman in *Just Tell Them That You Saw Me?*" He didn't speak for a long time and when he did, tears were merging with his rivers of perspiration.

"Carrie," he finally said, "the girl in that song isn't one of my sisters, it's two of them. Mame and Sylvia. Both of them gifted, strong. They were beautiful young women. Both had lost their way before they were twenty. They had nothing in their lives to keep them from giving in to their desires. Do you understand me?" He would never know how perfectly I understood him. I couldn't speak, could only brush his dampened cheek with fingertips that said yes, I understand.

"Sylvia," he went on, "I'm afraid Sylvia was caught up for a while" — he searched for the gentlest words, "in the *fancy* life. Mame was a high-priced doxy by the time she was sixteen and proud of it. Later on she lived with a married man and had his child. I blame myself and I blame my father. He was a tyrant, and a cruel one, God rest his soul. I left that Indiana farm behind me soon as I learned to sing and play the banjo — went out with a Medicine Show before I was fifteen. Maybe if I'd stayed home — I was the oldest — maybe I could have helped the girls, at least like I've been able to help my kid brother, Thee."

"Thee." That was his nickname for the sulky young reporter I had met in Amber's Chicago office several years before I met Paul. Let me tell you how that came about.

It was in 1902. My one-dollar folio *Seven Songs* was selling well, especially *I Love You Truly* and *Just a-Wearyin' for You.* I had urgent need to travel to New York about the latter song, to resolve the dilemma I described in Chapter Three: my rights to set Frank Stanton's poem to my music.

My nerve-rattling trip to New York that time, when I faced the first of my foolish plagarism follies, provided the unexpected opportunity to meet Paul Dresser. At the D. Appleton Company I agreed on terms to license the Stanton verse from them. (And somehow found the cheek to say I'd wager Mr. Stanton would make far more money from the song than he would from their little book of his poems.) Then I coaxed Mr. Appleton into recommending my work to some New York music concerns. Of course I had already formed my own publishing company in Chicago, but was hoping to gain better national distribution through a New York firm. By mail and wire I had recently solicited help from Mr. Kerry Mills of F.A. Mills, Inc., and from one of the Von Tilzer brothers — I forget which. I got the usual polite turn-downs. My songs were "too simple," "too difficult," "too artistic." Suddenly it was the 20th Century, so now I was "too old-fashioned!" "Really, Mrs. Bond, don't you have some coon songs? A ragtime ditty? It's all the rage."

Mr. Appleton scribbled a note and handed it to me. "Take this to Howley & Haviland at Four East 20th Street. I think one of them will see you." My heart almost stopped when he said the name of the firm. "Mr. Appleton," I said, "I thought it was Howley, Haviland and *Dresser*. Paul Dresser. Isn't he a partner?" "No, Mrs. Bond," he replied, "Dresser's been out for some months. He may be a fine songwriter, but they say he has a poor head for business. And I'm sure you've heard the other stories about him."

He sighed as if I must have heard "the other stories" and they were not to be discussed.

It was a long and tiring walk for me on that hot August afternoon, dodging the drays and hansom cabs and wishing I could afford to ride in one. I joined the New York women in raising our long skirts over the mounds of horse manure at every street-crossing, a maneuver I'd long-since mastered on the streets of Chicago. I stared in awe at the webs of steel and the mountains of stone and debris blocking great stretches of Broadway, as New York wrestled its railroads into the underground.

At the 20th Street office I could see that Paul Dresser's name had been scratched off the entrance, but recently. It still read "Howley, Haviland & — "

It was around two in the afternoon when I walked in. I handed Mr. Haviland my note from Appleton, looked down the hallway and saw that one of the offices was still labeled Paul Dresser. I'm sure I gushed.

"Mr. Haviland, does Mr. Dresser still use his office here?" I had forgotten all about pushing my songs. "I have always wanted to meet him."

Mr. Haviland invited me to take a seat in an empty cubicle. It was like an oven, strewn with sheet music and manuscripts and little else but a piano and a spittoon. I tried a chord or two on it, and it was terrible — out-of-tune, the ivory broken and stained, the tone like broken glass. I could see why they had begun to call this area Tin Pan Alley.

I would have much preferred to wait in the street —on the shady side. But I couldn't leave, not now. I waited until almost five, and Paul Dresser finally appeared. My first impression was one of great disappointment, almost shock. I had visualized him as an elegant, handsome man, of country origins, yes, but by now possessed of big city sophistication. Instead I was greeted by a hulk of unkempt man, probably three hundred pounds of him. He was dressed in what may have been a decent suit of clothes that morning, but by now the August heat and dust had reduced it an outfit befitting a hobo. His straw hat funneled a stream of sweat onto his shirt and collar.

In spite of this I must say I found him quite handsome. He moved with a grace that surprised me. He badly needed a shave, but I could see the strong nose and brow and the generous mouth that had surely contributed to his renown as a Lothario. He was smoking a cigar, and had obviously been drinking. And he could not have been more polite and charming. He kissed my cheek, then sang a few measures of *I Love You Truly* in my ear. "Mrs. Bond," he said, "I wish I had written it. It will make you rich." I didn't realize then how desperately he needed another hit song of his own.

He invited me to have supper with him, and I was thrilled to accept. We walked over to 23rd Street and into a tavern called Cavanaugh's. Thank heavens it had a wood-paneled cellar where it was at least a bit cooler. Upstairs and down it was crowded and noisy. Everyone greeted Paul, laughing, joshing him as he joshed them back. We were shown to a quiet rear table, whereupon he ordered a whisky and urged me to join him. When I told him I had never used alcohol, his manner was gracious, not snide and petulant like so many men in that situation. Everyone there seemed to know him, stopping at our table to gossip and talk about the new shows in town. We chattered on about New York and Chicago, the latest songs, the prospects of our new president, the first Mr. Roosevelt.

It was the beginning of a warm friendship that lasted until his death in early 1906. He ordered a light supper for us, and when we had finished he invited me to visit his lodgings at the Gilsey House. Without resorting to the doltish hints and winks that most men affect, he let me know, in a way that I can describe only as kind and respectful, that he wished me to be his partner for the night.

I think I replied with equal courtesy and restraint. I have never thought of myself as worldly in such matters, but I was, after all, a woman of almost forty, a veteran of two marriages and the several loving relationships I have revealed to you. But nothing in Paul Dresser's charm or my girlish admiration of him led me in this direction. I remember saying "no" to him in a voice as gentle as the one that had refused a fourth cup of tea. I was not embarrassed, nor, I'm sure, was he. Nothing he ever said or wrote to me from that moment on ever referred to our supper at Cavanaugh's and its tender coda. That big boy of a man just grinned, sweating still, put his warm hand on mine and said, "Tell me about the lucky man who inspired *I Love You Truly*."

I wish I could say Paul Dresser helped me to find a New York distributor. He did not, perhaps could not. I came to realize that during the few years left to him after he surrendered his partnership at Howley Haviland, he was no longer making a dime. He had produced twenty-five hit songs. They say at one point he was worth half-a-million dollars, but handouts to pals and poor folks plus lavish living took it all away. His biggest hit, one still very much with us today, was *My Gal Sal,* published just a few months before his death in 1906. Self-righteous critics smirked that "Sal" was not only an old flame of Paul's, but a former prostitute in Evansville, Indiana. Indeed she was, he once told me, and later a respected Madam — one true love among many others in his extravagant, storybook life.

Two or three years ago 20th Century Fox made a picture about Paul Dresser — a typical fairy tale of music and show business as seen by Hollywood. Victor Mature, an actor with a face and body almost surrealistically handsome, played Paul — in real life a Broadway Falstaff always in need of a shave, always perspiring, eating and drinking hugely at all times day or night, loving life and music as he first found them when he left home at fifteen. Lovely Rita Hayworth played Sal, now "Miss Elliott," in the picture. She couldn't be a prostitute — that wouldn't do. Sal was reformed into a young chorus girl struggling in vaudeville, helped, we are assured, by a gallant and lovesick Paul.

The script for *My Gal Sal* was written by his brother Theodore. I met this Dreiser brother again a few times in Los Angeles, and disliked him as thoroughly as I had upon our first meeting almost fifty years before in Chicago. He was by then the world-famous novelist, his big brother Paul a forgotten, somewhat foolish songwriter. Theodore died here in California, just a few days before I finished this account. Paul died so long ago that I am now free to say this: I think Paul was a great man, magnificent in failure and Theodore an arrogant and frightened success.

What is not known by those who have lionized Theodore Dreiser is that before he first won controversial fame with his book *Sister Carrie*, it was Paul who kept him going, bucked up his trembling spirit, "loaned" him money, created a magazine for him and appointed him editor-in-chief. Dear little "Thee" responded years later by claiming that he had written the words to Paul's lasting hit *On the Banks of the Wabash Far Away.* If Paul had lived to hear that, he would probably have said, "Oh, maybe so." He loved his little brother that much. But I can tell you this.

Without Paul Dresser you would never have heard of Theodore Dreiser.

CHAPTER 18

THE BOND SHOP

I have always tried to help young performers and composers — sometimes with money, but more often with a telephone call or a note to a producer or a manager I've come to know. Last year I gave a little boost to a young tenor you've heard on Jack Benny's radio program. Lots of young women have sought my help, including one who's become quite a star in the opera here and in Italy. I think many talented youngsters are afraid to "go to the top" for advice. I certainly was, in those bitter Chicago days. So I shall begin this chapter by saying, "Darlings, if you have dreams, don't hide in your room. Call on someone you admire. Chances are they'll help you, and if they won't, nothing's lost."

In my time of needing help, I was not a youngster, but a poverty-stricken 40-year-old widow in Chicago. I was nearing my wit's end as the century began. We had published a few songs, selling them directly to the stores around Chicago, but there was no sign of growth. I wanted to publish a folio. It would have my watercolor on the cover, with the title: *Seven Songs as Unpretentious as a Wild Rose.* Publishing it would cost five hundred dollars. I'd been doing my little ten-dollar recitals, and selling song-sheets each time. But I don't think we'd sold more a couple of thousand copies so far. I'd saved and saved, for a grand total of $250!

Victor Sincere was one of my new Chicago friends — a young attorney with a sweet tenor voice (and he *was* so sincere, and so handsome). One day he rattled me by saying, "Carrie, get out of these chilly rooms and take your songs to someone who will sing them — someone famous enough to excite the distributors and the recording companies. Jesse Bartlett Davis is back in town this week. Send a note or telephone to her. Do it!"

I was afraid. She was a star. I knew she was born an Illinois farm girl and came often to Chicago to visit her parents. But my goodness! She was now a fixture with the Boston Opera, and she was famous for the song *Oh Promise Me.* Everyone knew her!

Victor kept after me. "You've got to do *something*, Carrie." He was right. I cranked up my courage, and next day I went to the corner drugstore and telephoned to her. I was tongue-tied when Jessie Bartlett Davis herself answered, but I stuttered out my desire to meet her, in the hope she'd listen to my songs. I'm sure she was besieged by ambitious people — more, probably, than I am today, but I shall never forget her kind reply. "Would tomorrow afternoon be all right?" she asked. I struggled to hold back a sob of joy before I said, "Yes, of course. *Of course.*"

Next day she welcomed me at her home on Sutton Place, and after introducing me to her parents, led me into their lovely music room. Perhaps there was a touch of pity behind her kindness. I was very ill. It's a miracle I was even able to get there. My clothing was obviously homemade. If she noticed, she gave no hint. She seated me at a magnificent Steinway, and I did my seven little songs. At that time I had them only in manuscript.

"Mrs. Bond, these songs must be published at once," she said, "and my dear lady, I am going to sing them!" I know it sounds silly, but I nearly fainted for joy! But now came the hard part: the cost — five hundred dollars to print them the way I wanted. I told her I had only half that sum. She went right to her desk and scribbled out a cheque for two hundred and fifty dollars. "Get them to a printer as fast as you can," she said, "but not before we have some tea together." I have never forgotten the generosity of Mrs. Davis. She died in 1905 — only 46 years old. I hadn't known until I read her obituary that her husband was the controversial Will Davis — manager of the Iroquois Theatre at the time of the dreadful 1903 fire.

I was now my own publisher. When Jesse Bartlett Davis sang my songs, the newspapers would often print my titles in their reviews. Other singers took notice and orders began to pour in. *Seven Songs* was published as I had dreamed, with two of my "Three Songs" in it: *I Love You Truly* and *Just a-Wearyin' for You.*

My printer was Mr. Nelson, a fine old Swede said to be the best music printer in Chicago. He was a quiet, good-natured man who never once sent me a bill or asked me for a dime. After the Bond Shop finally began to prosper, he told me he always knew when I had the money I'd pay him. Mr. Nelson introduced me to my first "musical secretary," a young man named Henry Sawyer. He took down my music from dictation like a stenographer takes down a letter. I'd play a song for him just once and he'd have it. His manuscripts looked like engravings. We worked together for twelve years, and after I moved to California, I hired other "secretaries."

Bond & Son has long been known as a sound and profitable company in this risky business of popular music. But I learned many a hard lesson along the way. In those early years, I depended on Mr. Nelson's word about my account. I put my trust in him, rather than keep track myself. One fateful day I asked him what I owed him. He consulted his tidy ledger. "A little over fifteen hundred dollars," he said. My heart stopped, but not before I whispered, "I'll pay you, Mister Nelson, if it takes the rest of my life." "Whenever you can," he said.

The worst breakdown of my life followed. Frederic was away and I was alone — and desperate. I dragged myself to Christine Forsythe's sanitarium. "Just who," my editor Rose Ives said, reading this chapter, "is Christine Forsythe? You mention this 'dear friend of many years' only once in the old book. Tell us more."

Well, Dear Reader, you know how I treasure the love of my friends. Christine ran a small private sanitarium in Evanston. I had met her years before, when she was a night nurse at the grim County Hospital during my first stay. She was also a widow, with little income. We became close companions. In spite of our mutual poverty we spent many happy times together. Then her fortunes changed with an unexpected inheritance. It allowed her to buy the place in Evanston. It became an oasis for me of strength and health. Christine and I remained close for many years. I "loved her truly."

Her peaceful sanitarium had been a haven several times before, but this time, I told her, "I may have come here to die." In a dear, quiet room she sat with me for hours on end. She fed me and babied me as I poured out my self-pity — a forty-year-old woman, tired, in debt, sick, courting death. I saw that she was growing impatient with me. Almost scolding, she said, "Carrie, there must be someone you've known — some man of business who could help you and Freddie out with this."

"I've been too ashamed," I said. "None of my old friends even know where I live — or how I've struggled." But I thought back to Janesville, and remembered Cora Miller. We'd played together from the time we were three years old. Little Cora was there in the old smoke house the day of my accident. She had married and moved to Chicago. Her husband was Walter Gaines, a partner in a big drug company. I was shy about it, but Christine insisted I write to Mr. Gaines. Within the week he came up to Evanston, and we sat talking in the waiting room.

Walter Gaines, balding and bespectacled, was a bit brusque at first, probably resenting Cora's order to help a childhood friend. "My wife tells me you write songs," he said. "Do I know any of them?" I think I laughed and said, "No, but I'm hoping you will someday." A battered Kimball upright piano sat against the far wall. Without a word I went over, and looking him right in the eye, sang *Just a-Wearyin' for You* and *I Love You Truly.* He sat silent for a long moment. If he wasn't fighting back the tears, I'm sure there was at least a lump in his throat. "Cora has told me about Doctor Bond's death," he said. "Did you write those songs for him? "Yes and no," I said. "I consider myself a professional songwriter. I mean my songs for everybody."

His mood lightened, and within minutes the kind and practical Walter G. I've known for years emerged. "All right, Carrie—if I may call you that. I'll be blunt. Cora tells me you are ill and you are broke. Is that right?"

I told him I owed my printer fifteen hundred dollars. Right away he said, "Then you must be selling some songs to have a bill like that. What's gone wrong?"

"It's very simple," I said. "We're selling songs, but something's the matter. We're not making any money."

"Nothing's the matter," he said. "You just need some capital. Very few people could start a business with no money and come as far as you have." He pulled an envelope out of his coat pocket and did a little figuring, then said, "I will lend you the fifteen hundred dollars."

Now it was my turn to fight back the tears. But I had to say that I just couldn't borrow that much. What if I could never pay it back? "Just what would you say my business is worth?" I asked.

More figuring, then, "About nine thousand dollars," he said. I was swinging between shock and elation. "Then would you buy, say, a fifteen percent interest? That would be about fifteen hundred dollars." He went over to a little table and wrote out a cheque for $1500. "When can you have dinner with Cora and me?"

I left the sanitarium next morning. By noon I had endorsed the cheque over to an astonished Mr. Nelson. It was dated March 28, 1902. From that day on, until the deaths of these beloved friends of mine, they were both friends and family. I was often a guest at their beautiful home on Lakeshore Drive. Cora was often away, actively lecturing on behalf of the Suffrage Movement. Walter and I became very close for a time, but we never allowed this to affect our business relationship. He was my silent partner, Cora was like the sister I never had.

I call this chapter "The Bond Shop," shorthand to describe the years around 1901 to 1907 when success finally arrived for Bond & Son. Frederic left his job at the Burlington and came into our business full time. His health improved, and so did mine. (Wonderful how a little money puts roses in your cheeks.) Thanks to people like Walter and Mr. Nelson and Jesse Bartlett Davis, my songs were finally proving my fortune. So much happened in such a flurry of excitement and activity, it's hard to keep track.

Jesse's famous contralto had given my little songs their first big push, but it was a baritone who brought them to the full attention of the public. Not everyone today remembers David Bispham, dead since 1921. Those who do will recall that he was the first American-born singer to win international operatic acclaim. After one of his Chicago appearances, an increasingly fearless Carrie Jacobs-Bond out-waited the crowd backstage and pushed a copy of my *Seven Songs* into his hands. He was pleasant enough and said, "I'll let you know." A year went by. We had published another folio — eleven songs this time. We sent copies to his New York office. One day in the fall of 1904 I saw in the morning paper he was doing another Chicago recital. This time both Frederic and I pushed our way backstage. David Bispham put his arms around me and said, "Mrs. Bond. I have studied your songs. You *will* hear from me." A few months later I got this wire:

> RECITAL STUDEBAKER HALL APRIL 2ND. STOP. WILL SING FIFTEEN YOUR SONGS. STOP. WISH YOU TO ACCOMPANY ME. STOP. DAVID

Within a week his manager telephoned to us from New York. "There must have been some mistake," he said. Frederic read him the telegram. After he'd hung up, Frederic gave me a rueful smile. "The dear manager," he said, "has never heard of you. He thinks the concert will be a disaster."

The day of the performance I was ready to agree with him. Of the fifteen songs David had chosen, only one would be in the original key. I had to transpose the others to his keys. I somehow made my way to the piano that Sunday afternoon, certain my fingers would fail me.

They did not. I honestly believe I was in a trance — that the gifts and the confidence of my childhood returned to me. I had never heard such applause, nor have I since. I just sat there, glad I'd gotten through the fifteen pieces without a mistake. The applause went on. David finally tapped my shoulder and said, "You might want to stand up pretty soon, Mrs. Bond. This is for both of us."

Our applause certainly changed the tune of David's manager. He rushed backstage with hugs and kisses, and shouted," Carrie darling! You are made! You're a success!" David said, "Yes, but not just because of this afternoon." David, a Quaker, was one of the most self-assured, peaceful men I have ever known. When he died in 1921 the world lost a great voice, but an even greater person. And I lost a noble friend.

David's manager was right. The concert was on Sunday, April 2nd of 1905. Less than a month later, our sales had doubled. Frederic had mailed copies of the Chicago notices to newspapers and trade magazines all over the country, and to the big music stores in Chicago and New York. We decided to print *I Love You Truly* as a single sheet and it hasn't stopped selling since. Within two years we moved into our final Bond

Shop space on Michigan Avenue, with seventeen employees, shipping up to 40,000 sheets a month!

We bought back Walter Gaines' old thousand-dollar share. (He had made tidy profits on it.) A year later, at dinner one night with him and Cora, he said, "Would you sell me a tenth interest in Bond and Son again?"

I thought he was teasing. "Of course, Walter. How much is it worth this time?"

He dug in his pocket and handed me a cheque for $8,500. While I was putting my wits back together, he asked, "Do you know what you're going to do with it?"

I think I surprised all of us, myself included. "Yes, Walter," I said, "I know exactly. I'm going to buy another home in California and then go around the world!" And that's what I did. I bought the Pinehurst house in Hollywood, which I named "The End of the Road."

Then I took the longed-for, hoped-for journey — literally, around the world. Nearing fifty, this lucky lady became a seasoned traveler for the rest of her life. That story, Dear Reader, would require another book — one I know I shall never live to write.

I was becoming uncomfortably famous — and rich — but never by the way, the wealthy widow the world thinks I am. Perhaps if I had cared for money for its own sake, I might have been. But I lived in poverty for too many years. I can't turn away anyone who comes to me with a sad story. Stranger or not, they get whatever I happen to have.

In 1907 I was invited by President Roosevelt to appear at the White House! It was a small gathering at dinner, then a recital in the Blue Room. Joel Chandler Harris, better known as Uncle Remus, was among the dozen or so guests. So was the writer Finley Peter Dunne, a great friend of the president. By then Dunne was known by all as "Mister Dooley," but I remembered him as the brash young newspaperman I met that night years ago at the Bohemian Club in Chicago. By now, politicians and people in high places feared his sharp wit, while America chuckled. As we were getting into our coats he whispered to me in that Irish brogue of Mister Dooley's, "There's many a lad calls Teddy Roosevelt a fine fellow who would never think of votin' for him." I remember another Mister Dooley column — they were in all the Sunday papers for years — where he good-humoredly called Mr. Roosevelt the "rag-time president." And ragtime, oddly, takes me back to where I started this chapter: lending others a helping hand in the hard world of music publishing.

It was early in 1906. I was at my desk at the Bond Shop when a young woman came in and asked to see someone about publishing her music. She reminded me of myself not that many years before. I said, "Of course, I'm Carrie Jacobs-Bond. Please go over to the piano and sing something for me." She spoke right up. "Mrs. Bond," she said, "I don't write songs. I compose rags for the piano. Ragtime." I was at a loss. I didn't know a thing about ragtime. I'd heard the *Maple Leaf Rag* often enough the last few years, but had never tried to play it. It was far too difficult. The composer was a man named Scott Joplin. I didn't even know he was a negro, until one day I saw a picture of him on a piece of sheet music at Lyon & Healy's.

I asked my young visitor her name, and if she'd like a cup of tea or something. "No, thank you, Mrs. Bond," she said. "My name is Adaline Shepherd, and I'd like to play for you." I remembered how nervous I'd been, performing for a famous person. (No, I didn't yet think of myself as famous, but I'm sure she did.) Miss Shepherd sat right down at the piano and sailed into one of the most exciting pieces I'd ever heard — full of syncopated notes over a left-hand rhythm that never missed.

I was completely taken. "What on earth is that, Miss Shepherd? Does it have a name?" "I call it *Pickles and Peppers*," she said. "It's one of my rags. I've composed a lot of them." Miss Shepherd became "Addie" as we chatted, and I invited her to dine with me that night. Her home was in Milwaukee, she said. She'd been studying piano since childhood. Her teachers thought ragtime was trash, and beneath her. She said, "But I find it irresistible, intoxicating."

I had to tell her we published only my songs, but I had recently met a fellow right up there in Milwaukee who had a small company that took things for the piano, Mr. Joseph Flanner. I promised to write him next day that he must see her. Barely a month or so later she sent me ten handsome copies of *Pickles and Peppers* with its colorful cover of green pickles. It was very difficult. I spent an hour trying to play it until Frederic said, "Mother, *please!*"

I have no idea how he heard about it, but William Jennings Bryan, soon after he was nominated for president in Denver in 1908, chose *Pickles and Peppers* for his campaign march. John Philip Sousa said rags were just syncopated marches and should be played by a band. (He often proved that to be true.) It was certainly true for *Pickles and Peppers.* Hometown brass bands all over country played it for Mr. Bryan when he came through on the train. Addie Shepherd and I held hands as a huge band played it at a Bryan rally in Chicago that October. That great man came over and planted a kiss on her cheek. And on mine!

Mr. Bryan lost his run for President — again. But *Pickles and Peppers* sold 250,000 copies. Sad to say, I lost touch with Adaline Shepherd. She married a fellow named Olson, a rather wealthy man. Mr. Olson, according to Joe Flanner, didn't want his little wife wasting any more hours on ragtime.

CHAPTER 19

CALIFORNIA, HERE I COME

On the day I was finishing up this chapter, I heard a fellow on the radio named Johnny Mercer sing a new song called *On the Atchison, Topeka and the Santa Fe.* I came near borrowing it. You'll see why in a moment. I had already named the chapter, though, and I'm sticking with the Al Jolson song because it explains why I chose to live in this beautiful state for the last forty years: *"Where bowers of flowers bloom in the spring, each morning at dawning birdies sing and everything."* To this survivor of the deep snows in Wisconsin, the sub-zero nights in Iron River, and the windblown streets of Chicago, California was a paradise. It still is.

I worried I had to get permission to use the title. Rose, my editor, said not, but she'd check for sure. As usual, Rose knew what to do, and the very next day I had a telephone call from the fellow who wrote the words, Mr. Bud DeSylva. "Mrs. Bond," he said, "what a privilege to speak to you. I used to come by your Bond Shop on Highland when I was just getting started in the picture business out here, but you were never in. I wasn't sure —"

I think he started to say he wasn't sure but what I was dead. After I gaily assured him I was not, we had a lovely chat, ending with my question about getting Mr. Jolson's permission to use the title of his song. "Not necessary, Mrs. Bond," he said. "That's what we call 'fair use' in this business." He must have heard me breathe a sigh of relief, because he laughed. "I'll tell you a secret. Al's name may be on the sheet music of *California, Here I Come,* but he had nothing to do with writing it."

He must have thought me terribly naïve. "Why would you do that?" I asked him. "Why, Mrs. Bond," he said, "Joe Meyer and I were tickled pink to give Al a share. He sold a million copies for us. Same thing when Lew Brown, Ray Henderson and I wrote *Sonny Boy* for him years ago. His name's on that one, too. Another million copies."

I was charmed by Mr. DeSyla. "Next time you see Mr. Jolson," I said, "tell him he should make a record of one of my songs. He never has." "Okay," he laughed, "but I'll bet you won't put his name on it and split the royalties. I hear you are a very tough businessman." I let it go and didn't say business*woman* before I hung up. He'd been far too nice.

Now, about the Atchison, Topeka and Santa Fe. Believe it or not, I worked for the Santa Fe railroad for over six years. Rose tells me the song is from a new picture called *Harvey Girls*, and young Judy Garland is just wonderful. She says it's the story of how the Santa Fe hired Fred Harvey to provide passengers some decent food on those long trips. I know how much that meant. Starting in 1906, I made a dozen roundtrips on the Santa Fe from Chicago to Los Angeles, and I knew firsthand the joy of those sumptuous meals, served by the adorable Harvey girls all the way across the west. And whenever I could, I stayed at the Harvey House Hotels. To this day, even if I'm not traveling by train, I go out of my way to stop at a Harvey House. Sometimes with friends we motor over to Barstow just to spend a night at the lovely Casa del Desierto or to the El Garcas in Needles.

Do you find that life often connects unrelated events in mysterious ways? I do. When I was forty-five years old, my poor health connected me to a railroad, the railroad connected me to California, and California connected me to the creation of one of my most successful little songs, *The End of a Perfect Day.* Let me explain.

As you know I've been in-and-out hospitals a good part of my life, and Frederic's health problems in his youth were often nearly as bad.

We were beginning to see our way out of poverty in Chicago when Frederic went down again, spending weeks in the County Hospital. One day at a recital in Burlington, Iowa, I met a woman named Maud Perkins, whose husband was the president of the Chicago, Burlington & Quincy Railroad. We spent an afternoon together, and I revealed that my son had been very ill. "The doctor told me he must go immediately from the hospital into the country," I said. "He's getting well, but he's got to work out-of-doors for at least three months. He's only sixteen, but he's already trained as a civil engineer. We're hoping he can find some outdoor work with that."

"Why, Mrs. Bond," she said, "I think I can help you. The fact is, my husband tells me it's very hard to find qualified young engineers. I think the Burlington starts them at forty dollars a month." A small miracle for us! Frederic would still be in Chicago, but working for the Burlington, outdoors in the sunshine. And he'd still be able to spend time with his mother and the Bond Shop.

Several years later it was my turn to break down again, and I spent weeks in the Chicago Hospital (at least no longer on charity). My doctor was Alexander Ferguson, another of the gifted physicians threaded through my life. "Mrs. Bond," he said, "you must get away to a warmer climate. It's absolutely necessary." He'd done all he could. "It's up to you," he said.

Another railroad then connected to my life. Mrs. Perkins had sent a postcard asking how Frederic was getting along at the Burlington. I wrote back mentioning my own latest dilemma. She came over to Chicago the very next week and took me to meet one of her husband's business associates, a Mr. Busser at the Santa Fe. It so happened that they were just beginning a plan to provide reading rooms and gymnasiums for their workers along the lonely route from Chicago to California. "We're sending out musicians and lecturers to visit these places." he said. "They'll earn their transportation, then have a few days in California with all expenses paid. Would you be interested?" Maud Perkins and I could barely get out of his office before hugging each other with joy. "Carrie!" she said, "I'm going along on your first trip. What fun we'll have!"

We did have some good times — lots of card games and Chinese checkers, (my favorite). But my health was shaky, and the eight recitals in eight towns were a struggle. To make matters worse, I must have played on the eight worst pianos in America. Another recital was in the club car, en route. There was no piano, of course, so they hired a nice young man in Topeka to accompany me on the mandolin. He'd never heard of me or any of my little songs, but it didn't matter. All the men in the car had had so much to drink, they just took over. They joined in a dozen loud and tone-deaf choruses of *I Love You Truly.* Then three of them fought over who would escort me to my Pullman berth. The nice young man from Topeka saw to it I got to bed unaccompanied.

And so I was introduced to California, and Good Luck was waiting. Remember? The railroad connected me to California, California to music. The Santa Fe had reserved lodgings for me at the Hollywood Hotel. Chicago's famous soprano Genevra Johnston Bishop was singing there and arranging Sunday recitals. Madame Bishop knew of me through my dear friend David Bispham. She invited me to perform, and I continued to do so during the following visits, nurturing my Santa Fe-Hollywood Hotel connection. Each trip I spent more and more time at the hotel. Dear Mr. Busser didn't care, as long as I worked on a return trip.

So began my warm friendship with Margaret Anderson, who was the manager of the Hollywood Hotel when I first arrived — a charming hostess and brilliant at business, hired by the eccentric owner Myra Parker Hershey. The story goes that soon after the hotel was opened in 1902, the millionaire spinster Miss Hershey, (yes, the chocolate Hersheys) stopped in one day and was so taken by the cuisine, particularly the apple pie, that she fell in love with the place and bought it. She enlarged it to cover the entire block and added the famous ballroom, the wide lawns and cultivated gardens. People came from then-distant Los Angeles and Long Beach. They say the hotel helped to turn the tiny community of Hollywood into a town of its own.

I love the memory of old Hollywood — a beautiful place, but not much of a city twenty-five years ago! Our old neighborhood was a village of horse cars and dirt roads. There were a few lovely homes, among them Paul DeLongpre's, the painter. His magnificent corner on Hollywood Boulevard is now worth millions. No one dreamed of the Hollywood of today. The young men who would soon make it the movie capital of the world were still working in the soggy East, where there was no open country for making cowboy movies, and even worse, no *sun*. When news of California's sunshine reached New York, the rush began.

My second Hollywood home was the Beverly Hills Hotel, then an impossible nine miles west on Sunset Boulevard. Margaret Anderson and her son Stanley opened it in 1912. To this day it still feels to me like home, the minute I walk in the door. A hotel is supposedly a place where nobody much cares who you are or what you do, but here you felt as if you were a special guest. I lived there for months and was sure nothing in California could be more lovely.

But then some friends asked if I'd ever motored through southern California. So began a series of weekly motor trips: Elysian Park, Pasadena, and Riverside — for my first visit to the Mission Inn, where one "perfect day" a few years later would inspire my *Perfect Day* song. We visited Smiley Heights in Redlands. I toured their incredible gardens and met some members of the gracious Smiley family. They invited me, whenever I was in the East, to do a recital at their famous lodge in the Catskills, the Mohonk House. Many times I arranged to perform there when dear Elbert Hubbard was the lecturer. Times unforgettable.

We visited the Mission at San Juan Capistrano. Those old ruins are somehow more precious with every passing year. It was mid-summer, but I've gone back often in the month of March, when indeed, the swallows come back by the hundreds. I'll tell you a funny story. I once started to write a little song about the swallows, but I put it aside and forgot about it. Imagine my surprise — my pleasure, really — to turn on the radio a few years ago and hear those wonderful Ink Spot men sing *When the Swallows Come Back to Capistrano.* It was a big hit and composed, I found, also by a colored man by the name of Leon René.

After Capistrano we drove along a beautiful oceanside road to San Diego, and it was there I met two people who would become very dear to me — Colonel and Mrs. Ed Fletcher. After we spent the night in their lovely home, they drove us to "Grossmont" — a small mountain that Colonel Fletcher *owned*! There were tears in my eyes when we reached the 1300-foot summit and faced the distant ocean. It was sunset by then. How can I tell you the glories of that sunset? Think of the most beautiful colors you have seen in your life. They will be not half as beautiful. I was sure in an instant this was the one place in the world where I must live. The lot where we stood was for sale. I had enough money to buy it and I did, on the spot. My friends thought I had lost my senses. Frederic was convinced of it.

There are two massive boulders on the site, 40 feet apart. Col. Fletcher said he doubted a house could be built there. I said it could. My home would stand right between the boulders! That would be my living room, 29 by 40 feet. In my dreams for the next four years I built on that spot. I kept visiting, planning, measuring — picturing my house nestled between those majestic stones. First, I had to save up the money. Colonel Fletcher's man told me it would take $1,700 to build what I wanted — all redwood on the outside and lots of eucalyptus inside. My living room would have big, sliding windows, each one framing a priceless picture — God's pictures. I would greet the sunrise on one side, and on the other, watch the sunset from a great smiling porch.

"I've a cottage in God's garden, upon a mountain high,
Away from strife and turmoil and all life's din and cry,
The wild birds chant their carol, the wild flowers bloom galore
Out in God's garden. How could I ask for more?"

A pioneer neighbor at Grossmont was Madame Ernestine Schumann-Heink. When she learned I was to build, she had a lovely supper for me, inviting the Fletchers and William Gross. He said he was a "theatrical producer," but I guessed him a dilettante — one with lots of money. He made it clear he was the first to have owned the land, and named it *Gross*-mont. I found that terribly vain, and after Madame and I became friends, I shared the thought with her. She laughed. "Oh, Carrie," she said, "I tease him. I remind him that "gross" in German means "great," so we think of our homes on the "Great Mountain." Years later she bought Gross's own house as a gift for one of her sons.

Madame had seven children from three marriages. Several of her boys were in the war, including one in the German army. Because of America's anti-German madness at the time, the government suspected her of treasonable activities! They went so far as to post a few soldiers around her property to keep an eye on her. Not to be intimidated by Uncle Sam, she hired her own guards, and the two "armies" stared at each other across the property fence for a few weeks. The newspapers caught wind of it and ribbed the masterminds in the War Department, and they called off the watchdogs. Madame couldn't be bothered. She just laughed and went on entertaining our doughboys and raising money for them. She sold more War Bonds, they say, than any other person in America.

We became close friends. She loved my songs, and made a recording of *His Lullaby.* I sang it for her one day myself, and you can guess how shaky I felt with my little quiet voice, singing to a woman who possessed one of the great contralto voices of the ages. I understood why she didn't record more of my songs — they were simply not her style. She did sing a few — *Perfect Day* and *I Love You Truly* — on her programs after she'd become a radio star. I think the whole country was saddened when she died in 1936. We would never again hear her sing *Silent Night* every Christmas Eve.

I'm thumbing through my old Nest-o'-Rest guest book this afternoon — so many names, so many friends: Walt Disney, Pat O'Brien, Alec Templeton. Joseph Hofmann visited once. He said "This is like my home in Geneva, Mrs. Bond, but you have something even better. Privacy! You can work here and never worry you're disturbing anyone." Apparently his Swiss neighbors didn't appreciate his practicing — this man, this famous concert pianist. I am saddened to hear that Mr. Hofmann's playing has suffered in the last few years, due, they say, to his drinking. Somewhere I have a few of his early Duo-Art piano rolls — the "reproducing" kind that capture every nuance — not just the notes but the pedaling and the dynamics. I recorded some like that years ago for the Ampico Company — and quite a few regular piano rolls for the QRS people. It made me terribly nervous, and frankly, I don't think they're very good. I'm glad nobody I know owns a player piano any more. I certainly don't.

Chauncey Olcott and his wife occasionally paid me a visit. They always insisted on walking up to Nest-o'-Rest instead of riding up with old Mr. Jones in his one-horse shay for 25 cents. Chauncey was so funny. Here's what he wrote in the guest-book: "I lost my life coming up the hill, but spent a Perfect Day after getting up." That man had a magnificent tenor voice that could "hit the back wall," as they used to say, and did so on Broadway for many years. He said a touching thing to me about my songs. "Don't fret," he said, "if the critics call them folk songs. Be proud of it. Everybody knows your songs, Carrie, like they know mine — *When Irish Eyes Are Smiling* and *My Wild Irish Rose.* They sing our songs around the piano and around the campfire. They don't know who wrote them and they don't care — they just love the songs. And they *know* them. I'm proud of that."

Before he could get too sentimental, I said, "Yes, and they still make money, don't they?" He grinned. "Yes, Carrie, they do. That's why I'm living in Monte Carlo." The charming man died over there in 1932, but we still sing his songs. I hope we will for many years to come.

The names of Louis Bamberger and a Mr. Strauss are in my guest book together. I honestly don't remember Mr. Strauss's visit. I think he has something to do with Macy's. Louis Bamberger oversaw one of my first ventures into radio broadcasting. He founded radio station WOR. It's in New York now, but it was located over in New Jersey when he first asked me to come by as a guest. He had built one of the first real "department' stores in America, on Market Street in Newark. He was a radio pioneer, too, but he always said the only reason he started a broadcasting station was so he could sell radios at his store. In 1922 his first little studio was on the sixth floor of that huge place. (I could sing and then go shopping in the same building!) They moved the studios into New York City soon after that, but they always asked me to do a broadcast whenever I was in town.

How radio has changed since those primitive days! It's my best companion in my old age. I listen by the hour to wonderful music like the "Bell Telephone Hour" and the New York Philharmonic every Sunday. And I never miss the dramas — "The First Nighter from The Little Theater Off Times Square," or the "Lux Radio Theater," or "One Man's Family" which started up in San Francisco and has become a country favorite.

Another beloved star in my Grossmont guestbook is Amelita Galli-Curci, the Italian coloratura. This wise lady married her accompanist, Howard Samuels, and the three of us once stayed up past midnight at Grossmont, laughing and singing. Howard is one of those pianists who can play absolutely anything in any style. He once capped the evening by playing *I Love You Truly* for me as if Chopin had composed it, then Bach, then George Gershwin. What fun!

My Nest-o'-Rest was the second house built at Grossmont, or the third if you count Mr. Gross's original place. Then came Owen Wister

— the writer they say invented the Western novel with *The Virginian*. Their home had just been completed when his wife died in childbirth. It broke his heart, and he has never come back to Grossmont. Such a handsome, worldly man — he was a classmate of Teddy Roosevelt at Harvard. Here's a small-world note. Mr. Wister told me he had been among the guests at the White House when I did my recital for the President in 1907.

My deepest and most profound friendship from Grossmont was with Charles Cadman. He and his mother built a modest cottage, and he often said it was the one place in the world where he could forget Hollywood. We both have had homes in Hollywood too, but since the death of his mother, his has been a dreary hotel room in Los Angeles. I've been insisting that he move in with me at Pinehurst. He's such wonderful company — this man who composed two of the finest popular songs ever — *From the Land of the Sky-Blue Water* and *At Dawning* in 1906, far superior to the other so-called "Indian" songs from Tin Pan Alley like *Hiawatha* and *Red Wing*. Charles studied Indian culture seriously. He lived with the Omaha Indians for a year when he was a young man. He loved their odd melodies and harmonies, and made cylinder recordings of their music. Charles never married. The words of his songs were written by a childhood friend named Nelle Eberhart, whom he never mentions. He told me his youthful western jaunts had brought him back from tuberculosis, but his health now is very poor. I worry about him terribly.**

We try to see each other once a week, but it gets harder and harder. I suppose he worries about me, too. But after a life of illness, here I am still in one piece, where Charles, I fear, has given up on life. I may not have written any new songs lately, but I have constant friends, I have letters to write — and I have this book to finish. Rose and Jaime come by almost every day. Jaime scolds me about my dreadful long distance telephone bills, and I do spend at least an hour a day calling friends all over the country. It costs a fortune, but I refuse to change my habits.

I am blessed to have my Pinehurst "End of the Road" home in Hollywood, but it's been months since I've spent any time at Nest-o'-Rest. Jaime says we should sell it, but I have always found a reason to put it off. Both my homes seem such a part of me, and I can't imagine

** Editor's note: Charles Wakefield Cadman died on December 30, 1946, two days after Bond's death on the 28th.

my friends finding me elsewhere. Every "hand made" home has a soul. Mine still misses Frederic each day that dawns.

I never hear from Betty, but my granddaughters send me a postcard once in a while.

CHAPTER 20

VAUDEVILLE

"CARRIE JACOBS-BOND — THE GRAND OLD LADY OF SONGDOM!"

So said the sign outside a little uptown theater in New York where I was to "break in" my vaudeville act. I was 58 years old — a grand old lady, perhaps, compared with the talented young vaudevillians on the bill. But I insisted the sign come down. I was already in a terrible state of anxiety. I had missed the morning rehearsal with the orchestra, and never, in my hundreds of recitals, had I ever performed with an orchestra. So I called the agent, Mr. Weber, and told him I couldn't go on. It would have to be tomorrow.

"Are you ill, Mrs. Bond?" he asked. I explained that I'd missed the rehearsal. How *could* I go on? "My dear woman," he said, "you must, or you'll forfeit one thousand dollars."

So of course I went on. The sunny September day began as one of the most terrifying of my life, and ended as one of the most gratifying. The matinee became my rehearsal. There wasn't a big orchestra like I expected, just eight players. My piano on the stage was a fine

Chickering grand in perfect tune, and the wonderful young pianist in the pit must have been a mind-reader, the way he covered my mistakes. The blessed conductor was also the first violinist, and he smoothed over any stumbles the pianist missed. All the musicians smiled at me like old friends, and even applauded along with the audience after my first song. By the third show that night, when I took my bows and made my exit, I felt I'd become an "old pro," not that Old Lady on the marquee. A week later I was to make my full-fledged vaudeville debut, with a full orchestra, at a major Keith-Orpheum house. I couldn't wait.

Several months before, I had run across a letter in one of Frederic's files at the Bond Shop. It was from a theater up in Milwaukee, offering five hundred dollars a week for me to appear on their vaudeville bill. He'd said nothing to me about it, and I became as irritated at Frederic as I'd ever been — which wasn't often. I went to him and said, "Next time, my darling, let me make my own decisions."

"That came almost two years ago, Mother," he said. "I never dreamed you'd be the least interested. Quite surely your health wouldn't have allowed you to take on such a thing. And we certainly didn't need the money." I told him in no uncertain terms that I would have done it. "Frederic, your mother will soon be sixty years old. She is too comfortable, and far too set in her ways. She needs a challenge."

I telephoned to the theater that very day and asked to speak with a Mr. Halvorsen, the name of the letterhead. The first thing he did was to double the offer. "I apologize for not offering more at the time, Mrs. Bond," he said. "We are so very pleased with your recent successes. It seems your *Perfect Day* song is heard just about everywhere these days. Would you consider a thousand dollars a week?"

I was bowled over. I'm sure my voice was shaking. "Are you the person I should talk to about this?"

"We're part of the Keith circuit, Mrs. Bond," he said. "I'm sure they'll want to book you in lots of their other theaters. You'll need someone to handle affairs for you. There's a Mr. Humphrey in charge of their Chicago office, but let me suggest you meet first with Mr. Harry Weber in New York. He's a fine fellow and one of the best vaudeville agents I know of. I'll wire him at once."

Not an hour later a telegram came to the shop. I still have it:

Thrilled At Prospect Your Keith Bookings. Stop. One Thousand Minimum Guaranteed. Stop. Come New York Soonest. Stop. Harry Weber.

Amanda Blake was my assistant in those days. I had her ordering train tickets even before I told Frederic. Now it was his turn to be bowled over. "Mother, you mustn't think of it! You're too old. They'll expect you to perform twice a day — maybe three times. You'll be traveling constantly. You'll have one of your breakdowns sure."

I told him I'd probably break down if I *didn't* try it. I knew deep down inside I had to, because I could feel a fear, growing behind my excitement. I could feel the chill of stage fright creep up my spine — my mouth dry and my hands wet with perspiration, as on that dreadful night years ago when I had my one-night vaudeville try-out at Cole & Middleton's Dime Museum on State Street in Chicago.

I had done heaven knows how many of my little recitals by then — in private homes and hotels. But I had never been on a real stage in my life — not that Cole & Middleton's was anything like the beautiful vaudeville houses today. But it was a real theater, with a stage and footlights, a roll-drop curtain with ads for local businesses, two dingy dressing rooms, and seats for around five hundred. My dear Chicago companion Grace Boylan insisted on coming, sitting up in the gallery with Frederic to find out how my voice carried and cheer me on.

The upright piano they provided was a player-piano, at that time still quite a novelty. I had "cut" a few rolls of my little songs for these mindless machines, never dreaming I'd one day find myself on a stage *with myself* as my accompanist. I should have walked out! I was to sit at this player piano, pump it with my feet and sing my songs with it. In my recitals, I'd always kept my piano playing light and soft under my voice — still do. I should have known that after you've "hand played" a piano roll, the manufacturer adds to it, speeds it up, doubles some of the notes until it sounds like two people playing. I was about to be drowned out by myself!

When it came my time to appear, I think I just ran blindly out to the piano and immediately heard the gallery begin to hiss. I sang and pumped and tried frantically to fit my words to a clanging piano accompaniment I'd never heard before. I left the stage in full retreat, ran down Michigan Avenue with red-rouged tears running down my white vest. Right behind me were Frederic and Grace — Freddie with tears of his own saying, as he always did, "Mother you were just wonderful." They dragged me back to the Museum and there was Mr. Middleton, who said it was "splendid for your first time." My desperation returned when he said, "When you go on tonight it won't be half as hard." I told him he'd have to excuse me, and I vowed then and there I would never again appear on a stage. Nonetheless my heart fluttered when he handed me the cheque and said, "I wish it was for a thousand dollars instead of twenty-five."

My "never-again" was the kind of vow we sometimes utter because we cannot look ahead. Twenty years on, I became a vaudeville star — worth a thousand dollars, not twenty-five.

Barely a week after my vaudeville break-in uptown, I faced my real opening night at the Keith Theatre in Mt. Vernon, New York. At Mr. Weber's urging, a young singer by the name of Lois Bennett was hired to join me, and we had been rehearsing constantly. And yes, we had an orchestra rehearsal, and it was wonderful, a thrill. I thought my heart would burst, hearing the violins and woodwinds playing with us, harmonies I'd composed many years before. It was a big orchestra of over twenty players, with horns and tympani and a full string section. I fell in love with that conductor, too, and every one I've ever worked with since. Every man in the orchestra was polite and professional, and almost all of them said something kind to me — how it was a privilege to play for me, and how they loved my little songs. I had no idea whom Mr. Weber had hired to do the beautiful orchestrations. I certainly didn't know how to do it. I learned later on it was the work of Mr. Fred Vanderpool, very well-known in New York as a pianist and arranger. It turned out he was also the ASCAP member who never gave up insisting they admit me to membership — which they finally did in 1925.

There were 2000 people in the audience that September night at the Keith in Mt. Vernon, cheering with all their hearts. We heard it many times afterwards, but never like that opening night. They call it "stopping the show." I left the stage crying, where two stagehands supported me. One of them said in his inelegant but unforgettable way, "By God, Madam! By God, you've got 'em goin'!" My lovely little red-headed Lois shared the applause, with bow after bow. My first concerns about her — so young, totally unfamiliar with my songs — were washed away. Her light contralto was just right, and critics loved what one called our "mother-daughter" look. Another critic wrote, "It was different from any 'act' vaudeville has had. Sweet lavender and old lace were delicately and subtly suggested by the personal appearance of the snowy-haired Mrs. Bond and the demure and ingenuous Miss Lois Bennett…with a voice of wondrous sweetness and plaintive tenderness…" Yet another said "We made even a cold Monday matinee audience seem human. Mrs. Bond is not merely a famous woman; she is an entertainer whose act would stand without the lure of a name." Was this "snowy-haired" woman pleased, thrilled by all this praise? You bet your bottom dollar she was. By then I'd read every level of good and bad reviews of my songs, but never on myself as a performer.

Musically, I was in heaven. Physically — Frederic had been right. By the end of the first week I was near exhaustion. Mr. Weber, with Frederic on the long distance half-dozen times, arranged for a trained nurse to be with me twenty-four hours a day. The woman they hired — dear Miss Bea Gilbert (my "Gillie") — was everything to me. I couldn't have gone on without her. She was never distraught, and she took care of me every time I was ill. Which was often.

One of our most memorable nights was in Providence — a Midnight Performance on election night, November 2nd, 1920. Women had finally gotten the vote! Lois and Gillie and I were far from home, so we couldn't cast our first-ever votes, but I'd have voted for Harding and Coolidge rather than Cox and Roosevelt. I didn't know it then, but Mrs. Harding and I would become friends. I visited them twice at the White House. Looking back I suppose I should have supported Cox and Roosevelt, but I had lost faith in the Democratic Party after President Wilson took us into the war. Who would have guessed then that twelve years later, Franklin Roosevelt would become the president who would lead us through the Depression and the next war, only to pass away just months before we would celebrate the end of it.

The Bonds and the Jacobses had always been dyed-in-the-wool Democrats and as you know, I adored Mr. Bryan, and voted for him all three times. I think he was one of the few politicians who truly thought he should help the workers and the poor. I suppose he really believed Prohibition would be good for the country but I couldn't see any sense in it. I was heart-broken when he went through that degrading "monkey" court case in Tennessee just before he died — of a broken heart, I've always thought.

Mr. Weber and his lady friend and several people from the Keith-Albee office came up from New York that election night. There was quite a party at the hotel. I had a bit of wine and went on to bed, but Lois and Gillie stayed late and said there was lots of whisky and gin as the evening wore on, although Prohibition was nearly a year old. It has always seemed curious to me that America started woman suffrage and Prohibition the same year. It seems women have been blamed ever since for Prohibition, in spite of the fact we didn't get the vote until after it began.

The next six months are a blur of dressing rooms and Pullman cars, parties and exhaustion, and moments of pure joy. We played half-dozen of the big Keith houses in the East: Providence, Pittsburgh, Boston. Mr. Weber had arranged for me to have a week off every month, which may have saved me from a complete breakdown. I won't play Carrie the Perfect here, like I did in my other book. I was in pain a good part of the time, and many a day I came close to quitting. Nurse Gillie kept after me to eat right and get my rest, and her loving hands gave me daily massage that sometimes kept the pain at bay.

I did finally give it up, of course — not that I couldn't any longer, but that I *had done it*! My 60-year-old body said it was time to go back to California and write songs and be with friends, and return to other endeavors that I'd forsaken for the "Show Business." Frederic and Betty had urged me to quit weeks before. A thousand dollars a week, Frederic said, was nice. But Bond & Son was netting twice that much every week, with no signs of slowing down. "The country's got a new president," he said, "and we're heading into a prosperous time, now with the war over and the Republicans back in office." His prediction held true for the rest of his years on earth. He died almost a year before October, 1929.

Frederic had to admit the vaudeville tours were good for business. In every city I appeared sales of our sheet music and recordings would soar. The piano roll companies saw the same spurt in business. Mine did well enough, but rolls of my songs that Felix Arndt made for Duo-Art sold like hotcakes. Such a loss, that dear young man, one of the thousands that died of the dreadful influenza in 1918. People still play his wonderful *Nola*, which I dearly love but find far too difficult ever to master.

My vaudeville days produced a flood of newspaper interviews and articles. I'm not much of a pack rat, but Frederic was and so is Jaime. There are bulging scrapbooks here at Pinehurst I hadn't looked at for years. I've been going back to them, and am both amused and shocked by some of the things I said, or they *said* I had said. I did warn you in my first chapter that I have cautiously but intentionally lied about some parts of my life. The Boston *Post* quoted me in their pages on November 12, 1920, telling of "...my marriage while only a girl to a young doctor..." Yes, that's the story I was telling. The truth, of course, was that I was twenty-six when I married Frank Bond. I was "only a girl" when I married Edward Smith eight years earlier. All the years since, I have purposely edited that sad chapter from the scrapbook of my public life. In the *Post* article I go on to say: "For several years we lived in the glorious outdoors of Northern Wisconsin [it was actually Michigan]...From this outdoor life came the inspiration of many of my songs. Then the arrival of a small son suggested lullabies."

Yes, I probably did say that. Our "small son" was way beyond lullaby-time when Frank and I married, but it made for a better story. Frederic was actually eight years old when he was finally united with his real father. I did write a few lullabies in those days, but only because a couple of hard-headed Chicago publishers thought they'd be the "suitable" thing for a woman to compose.

That interview was published just after the November election — a first time for the woman voter. So I was asked what I thought about all that. Here's what they said I replied. "I am a firm believer in women's rights...and I also am of the opinion that a woman can have a career and a happy home too. But if she finds she cannot have both I'd advise her to chose the happy home."

Another lie. I must have thought it best to provide the expected answer for the times. I'd had two marriages. The first was a wasteland. The second — heaven on earth — had ended years before. If I'd been longing for another "happy home" ever since, I would have found one. My friends and my family had long ago given up pushing me toward this or that promising suitor, so that I could again enjoy a "good marriage." Let me tell you — I've never met a man since Frank Bond who could have persuaded me to give up the rich, independent life I've led. You know by now of the cherished friendships and the loving relationships I've had all these years with both men and women. I haven't needed or wanted a husband to tell me what to do and where to go. Granted, I've been able to pay my own way. I'm well aware that most women can't do that, but it's easier now than it used to be. So yes, my dears. If you've been on the marriage-go-round and want off — or have been pushed off — I say quit looking for that "Happy Home." Build one of your own.

CHAPTER 21

A SONG IN MY HEART

My earliest memory is not of a place, a word, a face. It's a scrap of melody. Do you remember your do-re-mi's, your *solfeggio*? My melody is this: sol-fa-mi/mi-re-do/ re-do-re-mi-sol. If you can hear notes in your head or have a piano handy, in the key of C it's G-F-E/E-D-C/D-C-D-E-G. It was to be the first melody of hundreds that, throughout my life, would enter my mind unbidden.

Sometimes they stay away in the back, as when I'm dealing with practical matters, or struggling with my illnesses, or when I've simply "got the blues." But they're always there, and I write down the ones I like best. (Many of them are now bringing good returns to Bond & Son, Inc.) Until I was eight or nine years old, I assumed everyone else had a song ringing in their head like I did, same as breathing. But when I finally began my piano lessons, my teacher laughed and said he'd never heard of such a thing. "Of course, Carrie," he said, "musicians often have a melody ringing in their ears, but it's someone else's melody — something from an opera. Or a hymn." I tried to tell him mine were different. "Nonsense," he said, "the untrained mind alone cannot produce original melodies."

I have asked other songwriters about it, several generations of them, and not one of them qualified. I had put the question to my dear Paul Dresser years ago. Since then I've known a few of the professionals here in Hollywood well enough to ask about it — men like Harry Warren and the late Ralph Rainger. Most reply something to the effect that to write a song, you get out a blank piece of manuscript paper, scan the words you or your partner has scribbled, and *construct* a melody. It is simply a craft, they insist, and they are very good at it. Heaven knows Mr. Warren, Mr. Rainger, and my dear-departed Paul Dresser have created wonderful songs without the "gift." Perhaps a melody in the head all one's life is a curse rather than a blessing.

One day when I was almost sixty, my eye fell upon a poem in a copy of *Good Housekeeping* magazine, of all places. It was called "Little Lost Youth of Me". In a breathless moment I realized the words of the title fit my childhood melody perfectly! And the next line —"where are you roaming," continued to match my notes — re-do-mi-sol-fa or D-C-D-E-G. Within an hour I had fleshed out the entire poem as a song. It's been my favorite ever since, because it brought back to life that haunting tune of childhood memory. We published it in 1923, and I was even inspired to revive my custom of painting in watercolor a wreath of roses for the cover. It sold only moderately for a year or so, but the poem, now a song, spoke for an ageing dowager (I was sixty-one), surrounded by wealth and glamour and dozens of friends, visiting her "little lost youth" (me again), much of which was spent in poverty and pain.

Little Lost Youth of Me, where are you roaming,
You who were part of me only today?
Why did you slip from me out in the gloaming,
Little lost youth of me, vanished away?

Little lost youth of me, why did you leave me?
You of my life were so lovely a part!
Long will the wraith of you haunt me and grieve me,
Little lost youth of me, slipped from my heart.

The poem was written by an Eleanore Myers Jewett, one of my silent partners in writing songs. I've told you of others — famous poets like Frank Stanton and the haunted negro genius Paul Lawrence Dunbar. Mrs. Jewett of course was not well-known, and I tried in vain to reach her and thank her for those verses, but my letters went unanswered. I longed to know if her poetry spoke of her own life. Was she expressing heartache for vanished years, as have I, in so many of my own poems and songs?

I wonder if you have read Alexander Woollcott's biography of Irving Berlin? It was published in 1926, just a year before my *Roads of Melody.* I didn't think it proper to quote from it at the time, but I wish I had. Mr. Woollcott declares that Irving Berlin possesses the gift — if that's what it is — that he too always has a new melody running in his head. Mr. Berlin himself slyly confirmed it to me not too long ago. "Doesn't everybody?" he grinned, knowing it wasn't so. We were chatting during a gala we both attended at the Pasadena Playhouse. I had met him once or twice before in Hollywood, but never with time to really talk. I took the opportunity to ask him that question songwriters always avoid: is his own life in his songs? I was sure it was — at least early in his career — but he rarely owns up to it.

"Mrs. Bond." He kissed my cheek. "What a pleasure to meet the only person in our business besides me that owns all their own music. How'd you do it?" It was a sincere question. I knew that Irving Berlin was as good a businessman as he was a composer. He was honestly curious. "Mister Berlin," I said, "when I was starting out in Chicago, with no money and small hopes, I would have rushed to sign away half or all of my royalties to anyone who'd ask. Nobody asked."

He grinned, "I'd have asked." He was delightful. I teased him back. "But you weren't around. I think you were still singing for nickels and dimes on the Bowery."

"And you were burning the furniture in Chicago to keep you and your little fellow warm. I've read your book. What about answering my question?"

"Mister Berlin," I said, "by the time the big Chicago publishers began courting me for my songs, I had learned all I needed to know about the music business, and had incorporated Bond & Son Publishers. I own my songs."

He has a wonderfully tough New York way of speaking. "Here's to you, darling. You beat 'em at their own game. By the way, I wish I'd written *I Love You Truly*. Bet you've made a pile on that one." I saw my chance to ask him that question — did he write some of his songs from his own heart. "I've made it known it was composed in memory of my husband," I said, "much like you wrote *When I Lost You* when your first wife passed away so suddenly. That is so, isn't it?"

"Perhaps," he said. He paused in silence for a long moment, then nodded, "Yes, it's so." He turned away, then teasing again — "But if you quote me in your column, I'll deny it." He took my hand in his. "I didn't intend to make money with her death, and I'll bet you didn't with his. Good night, Mrs. Bond."

CHAPTER 22

FIRST RECORDING AND LAST CONCERT

Somewhere at the Grossmont house I have a set of the recordings I made for the Columbia company in 1915. As I recall it was called something like American Columbia in those days, before the broadcasting company bought it and changed it to plain Columbia Records. I didn't want to bother with it, but Frederic insisted it would be good for business. "Everybody's making them, Mother, and you need to get it done." I thought why should I do it? Dozens of others were recording my music. My dear neighbor Henrietta Schumann-Heink had recorded *Just a Wearyin' for You* for the Victor Company, and then, because I asked her to, *My Lullaby.* She said afterwards that she loved that one too, and wanted it for her grandchildren. Those old Victor records seem so scratchy and ancient now, compared to the beautiful strains we hear from our Victrolas today.

My contract with the Columbia people said they'd put me on their cylinders and both sides of their flat records — they were still doing both. But they never released them, and I think I know why.

Singers today have no idea how recordings were made in those days. Before the microphones and all that were invented, people with small voices (like mine) hadn't much of a chance. Believe me, a lot of singers who are today's stars wouldn't have gotten in the door. You had to have a big opera voice like Caruso's or Madame Schumann-Heink's, or one of those tireless vaudeville voices — remember Billy Murray? Or Ada Jones? My voice was never strong. I have no idea how I managed to be heard in those cavernous vaudeville theaters a few years later. (I guess people just tried harder to listen.) But there I was in 1915, invited by the Columbia people to come to New York simply because now I was "famous." They stood me in front of the huge megaphone (yes, *megaphone*, not microphone) to read my poems. I did some of my "Old Man" pieces and the "Little Boy's Lament," — just speaking them. You see, earlier in the week, the young Columbia fellows had tried getting me to sing while I played the piano, like I always do. But I had to keep bringing my mouth closer and closer to the megaphone, until they couldn't get a note from the piano. So finally they said, "Mrs. Bond, we're sure the public would love just to hear your voice. Let's do that today." So we did. And you may know, they never put those records on sale. They paid me, of course, but nothing came of Frederic's dream of Mother's phonograph records selling more of our sheet music.

Then there was the matter of lost income from the recordings themselves. Frederic explained that when the Congress passed a new copyright law — 1908 or nine, I think — it made the record companies pay for using our music. (And piano roll companies too, thank heavens. I'd made a lot of those.) It amounted to two cents for each song per copy, which was a lot in those days. (And by the way, it's still just two cents, even with everything else going up since the war.) Frederic told me about that glorious soprano Alma Gluck making a record of the old song *Carry Me Back to Old Virginny* for the new Red Seal records. It sold a million copies. That would be $20,000 in royalties, he said. (Paid to the composer and the publisher, not Madame Gluck, although I'll bet by then she had a good lucrative contract with the Victor Company.) If Mr. James Bland, the composer, had been alive, it would have meant $10,000 if they split as usual, half to the composer and half to the publisher. "But think, Mother!" said my Frederic. "We are both! You are the composer and we are the publisher! We'd get both halves!" My boy was very persuasive when it came to money. He was right, of course. If we could have sold a million of something, Bond & Son would have gotten every nickel of that $20,000. Too bad my records never saw the light of day. Of course, we do get "both halves" when someone else sings my songs.

I wonder who got all that money from poor Mr. Bland's song. His little publisher in Boston I suppose had long ago closed up shop. As a colored man, I don't think Mr. Bland would have had much luck getting paid after all those years, even if he'd been there to try. He died in 1911, tubercular, they said, and down on his luck. I had always admired his music and heard him on vaudeville bills — once in Chicago around 1902 and later in Milwaukee. I could see why he'd been known as one of the greatest of the minstrel men, but by then he was failing badly. I greeted him briefly backstage and he responded warmly, a quiet, dignified man who had graduated from Howard University and then lived in London for many years. I longed to talk with him about his songs, but his wife saw to it that he got his nap between performances. People called him "The Black Stephen Foster," and he wrote hundreds of songs, including one of my favorites that we all still love to sing around the piano — *In the Evening by the Moonlight.*

That old copyright law is still with us. It couldn't possibly have covered all the changes in the music business since then. How could Congress have known, for instance, about a thing called radio? It changed forever the way our music is heard and sold. How would we get paid for it? The copyright law had nothing to say about that. That big step came a few years later, and this time not from Washington, but from New York — with an organization called the American Society of Composers and Publishers — ASCAP. It was founded in 1914 by people like Victor Herbert and Gustave Kerker and one of the Witmarks. No one, they said, was paying attention to a line somewhere in the copyright law that said songwriters should be paid when their music was "performed in public for profit." Congress obviously meant on recordings and piano rolls, but ASCAP insisted it also meant composers and publishers should also be paid whenever their music was *performed* someplace — any place using music "for profit." They've had many a hard fight to convince, say, a night club owner that if his dance band played *Star Dust* or if Bing Crosby sang *I Love You Truly* on his radio program, Hoagy Carmichael and Carrie Jacobs-Bond should get a few pennies for their trouble. But now we do! It adds up, and we've been cashing those nice ASCAP checks every quarter. Since 1925.

If you're bothered by the nine-year gap between when ASCAP started out and when I became a member — so was I. ASCAP, led by a decent fellow named Gene Buck, has been known from the beginning to welcome negro songwriters. I've wondered why, if the ASCAP door was open to colored men (as of course it should have been), it wasn't just as open to women, including this one. Negroes like Andy Razaf, Eubie Blake, and Spencer Williams became members right away, after their first successes. That great gentleman James Weldon Johnson, who helped me straighten out my silly mistake using Mr. Paul Dunbar's poems years ago, was a charter member, and they say until the day he died he worked behind the scenes to keep things fair and equal.

I honestly hadn't paid much attention to all this until I performed in the ASCAP Cavalcade of Music Concert in 1940. I shall never forget it — 15,000 people in the Coliseum on Treasure Island up in San Francisco. Mr. Buck was the Master of Ceremonies. Jerome Kern and Harold Arlen and Harry Armstrong (who sang his *Sweet Adeline*) were there. I think at seventy-eight I was the oldest performer on the bill, six years older than that rascally ham Joe E. Howard. He had strutted through an unrehearsed cakewalk and came off to rousing cheers, always chasing applause and chasing the ladies too. After the concert Mr. Howard made over me — how he loved my songs and how he wished he had met me "in the old days." He had sung *I Wonder Who's Kissing Her Now* and some other song for an encore, but not his *Hello, Ma Baby* from way back in 1899. I told him it was the first time I'd ever heard the word "ragtime" in a song ("...hello, ma ragtime gal..."). He laughed and said he thought then it was just a catchy word for a passing fad, but the young folks would like it.

I had tea with darling Ann Ronell. She'd become an ASCAP member eight years earlier with her song *Willow Weep for Me.* I told her it was one of the most unforgettable songs I'd ever heard and asked her who wrote the words. "I wrote the music and the words, Mrs. Bond, just like you do." Well, from then on we were Ann and Carrie. She told me how she'd gone through the usual difficulties of getting published when she came to New York from her hometown of Omaha, but that Irving Berlin's company had published the "willow" song, and that he wasted no time getting her into ASCAP. I don't think she minded when I said I wished Mr. Buck had asked her to play that one, instead of her silly little *Who's Afraid of the Big Bad Wolf,* from the "Three Little Pigs" cartoon. She told me she really hadn't written it at all — had just added some words at the last minute. But the ASCAP people, she said, thought it would be "cute" of her, and she rolled her eyes. That's when we got right into the subject of women in popular music.

I asked if she knew some of the other composers of her generation — Kay Swift, for instance, and Dana Suesse — so talented. "Things are a little better than when you were young, Carrie," she said, "but it's still uphill for women." She told me about Rida Johnson Young and Beth Slater Whitson. They weren't admitted to ASCAP until years after they died! Their songs had ended up in somebody's huge catalog, she said, and the publishers got the dear dead ladies admitted to ASCAP to get half the royalties.

I hadn't known much about Mrs.Young, except that she'd written the words to *Mother Machree,* with music by my friend Chauncey Olcott. But I had met dear little Beth Whitson when she came up to Chicago from Tennessee with her simple poems. A man named Lou Friedman set them to music, paid her fifteen dollars for the first one and sold it outright to Will Rossiter Music for seven thousand dollars. That was in 1909, when Bond & Son was sitting on top of the world in Chicago, publishing just my songs. We had never published anyone else's, but I told Miss Whitson that if we'd known about her, we would probably have taken that first song *Meet Me Tonight in Dreamland* — such a huge success — and we would certainly have paid royalties to her.

Her next song, *Let Me Call You Sweetheart,* went to Rossiter's little brother Harold, who treated her better, I'm told. She was a beautiful young woman, so shy, scared to death of Chicago and its big-city bustle and noise. I heard from her a time or two after she'd gone home to Tennessee, then lost touch until her sister Alice, by then a successful poet and writer herself, wrote that Beth had been committed to an insane asylum and died there in 1930. Beth Slater Whitson wrote the words of two of the biggest hits ever in popular music, but she never became a member of ASCAP.

George Cohan and Irving Berlin closed the San Francisco concert — which was free to the public, by the way. What ovations they got! Mr. Cohan told the audience that Jimmy Cagney was starting work on a picture about his life and he hoped he'd live to see it. He did, just barely, and Mr. Cagney won an Academy Award for it. It made me wonder if I'll live to see the picture about my life that Mr. Keighley is going to make. I'm not sure I care.

Mr. Cohan sang a couple of his patriotic songs and then Irving Berlin walked on stage and in his creaky little voice did his new song *God Bless America*. It had just come out the year before, but it seemed like Kate Smith had been singing it on the radio once a week, and everybody knew the words. The audience began to sing with Mr. Berlin. 15,000 voices! Let me tell you, I finally knew what they mean when people say their hair stood on end. Go back to that September in 1940. The Nazis were in Paris and the British were fighting for their very lives. It was a dark time. Our patriotism, I remember, was heated-up by a mixture of pride and fear. And it found a voice in *God Bless America*. A better curtain to that concert couldn't have been planned. Thank heavens I can write now in prayer and thanksgiving that this horrible war is over, and the world can look forward to peace at last.

Mr. Buck had asked me to compose a new song for the concert. I called it *The Flying Flag* and it got an ovation too — due, I fear, more to patriotism than to the song. I can't say it's one of my best, and to make matters worse, it was sung by a tenor named Allan Lunquist, booked by ASCAP. He had just sung my *Perfect Day* with a very nervous me at the piano. Mr. Linquist, I'm sorry to say, is one of those tenors who think their golden tones are all that's necessary to sell a song. It's a wonder the microphone didn't just melt away. I tried to keep him going, but he dragged out *Perfect Day* like a dirge, and he did the same with *The Flying Flag*. I was so embarrassed that I made a terrible mistake on the piano introducing the flag song. Thanks heavens the concert wasn't being recorded. ***

*** Editor's note: Years later it was discovered that acetate recordings of the concert indeed had been made. They have since been released in a boxed 4-CD set by Norbeck & Peters, Woodstock, NY.

CHAPTER 23

FREDERIC

"Sometimes when shadows cross my path;
As shadows sometimes do,
I reach my hand across the mist and touch the hand of you.
The dearest memory of my life, I touched the hand of you,
Please God, let me still touch the hand of you…"

My beloved Frederic left this earth seventeen years ago. I was told he died by his own hand. For weeks I refused to believe it. They found him in our cottage at Arrowhead. There was a gun. I insisted it had to be the act of an intruder. My friends and the police told me there was no question.

I first thought I'd write of this most agonizing event of my life by avoiding it. One sentence would do. "At age forty-seven, my son Frederic Jacobs Smith took his own life." But I can't leave it that way. Words have poured out beyond my control. Tragedy has often been my lot, but the loss of Frederic has been the hardest to bear. He was my friend, my partner, my greatest love, my *life.* Each day I expect his telephone call. In the quiet at Pinehurst I talk to him about my day and ask his advice. My words in *Roads of Melody* haunt me: "Everybody who has a child in this world knows the great joy, or the great sorrow that they can bring, and mine has brought me only comfort." One year, almost to the day I wrote that, he was dead.

There was talk he had a cancer. If he knew of it, he never said. Frederic often had stomach trouble as a child. We had no idea why. He probably had allergies, but in those days no one knew about that. We loaded him with peppermint and paregoric, and when that didn't help, we forced a spoon of castor oil down the poor child. Maybe there was a cancer even then, and he overcame it. At fifteen, when he was working day and night with me in Chicago, Frederic lost a whole month in the grim County Hospital, fighting just to keep his food down. (I hope today's readers understand that "County Hospital" meant charity.) Perhaps it was appendicitis, but appendectomies hadn't become commonplace like they are today. It could have been an ulcer. I'm told that doctors now believe such things are brought on in childhood by worry and dread, but I refuse to believe that with my Frederic. Through all our ups and downs — the early, mean years with Edward Smith, our divorce, the move to Iron River away from his school friends, then into our Chicago poverty — I did all I could to make my boy happy. He told me every day how much he loved me.

Frederic's widow, Betty, has blamed me since that awful day for holding him back, for "hounding him," as if he'd no choices in life. I've told her my dear child *wanted* to help his mother and often spoke of treasuring our closeness as deeply as I did. But she succeeded in planting doubt, and has driven me to wonder if I failed him in some way.

When his father died in that stupid accident in Iron River, Frederic came to me next day, put his arms around me and said, "Mother, darling, I can do something for you. I can be as kind as doctor always was, and I always will be." It was terribly careless of me to write in my other book that he was only nine years old that day. He was fourteen, of course. Betty points to that silly mistake as proof that I babied Frederic all his life. If he were alive today I'm sure he would tell her there's no stronger bond in this world than that of mother and son. His first wife, sad to say, failed to understand this, which may have led to their early divorce. I regret that Betty Smith has also had difficulty reconciling Frederic's obligations to his mother with his devotion to her. The tension has continued to this day, and has driven a wedge between us, and even between my darling little granddaughter and her loving grandmother.

Frederic died in that lonely cabin on December 28, 1928. The newspapers made great play of the fact that a recording of the *End of a Perfect Day* was still spinning on the Victrola when they found him. Some chose to interpret that as a parting rebuke to his mother. I must believe it was just the opposite — a final tribute. But there was a meanness in some of the newspaper stories. *The End of a Perfect Day?* one said. Why wasn't it *I Love You Truly*? I didn't know of this gutter reporting until weeks later. I died a death of my own that December day. Dr. Marshall took charge and hurried me into isolated hospital care. I have almost no memory of the weeks that followed, except for nights without sleep, followed by days of dark slumber, probably the result of the potions Dr. Marshall prescribed. You'll read in my closing chapter how I found, miraculously, the strength and the desire to return to my daily life by early summer of 1929. But I was slow to return to Hollywood's pace. Dear Esther Fairbanks, without my asking, had simply taken over the avalanche of mail and telegrams at Pinehurst, and cared for my dear pups Mike and Pooch.

Sales at the Bond Shop went on without Frederic and without me, but thank heavens we no longer had to actually fill and ship orders from all over the world. Turning over distribution of my songs to Gustav Schirmer's Boston Music a few years before was a greater blessing than we could have imagined. I'm sure I'd otherwise have faced a rash of settlements and lawsuits for non-deliveries and broken contracts.

There was the question of Frederic's estate. I knew his other investments had not been going well. I learned that he'd drawn a separate will unknown to me, leaving his holdings in the candy store and the box business to Betty and their little girl, and to his daughter Dorothy from his first marriage. I was shocked and hurt to hear this, but decided perhaps his failing health had affected his judgment. I didn't want to believe it was pressure from Betty — or who knows what unknown business partners — that made him hide this from his mother.

I think Betty always resented that I didn't encourage Frederic to become a doctor. She said it had been his great ambition. His father — in his eyes, his step-father — was a physician and so were both his grandfathers. He spent seven years in Iron River, where every minute away from school he'd be around the doctors' office or downstairs in the drugstore, soaking up the language of medicine. Mother always said too, that Frederic should be a doctor. Years later he finally confided in me that he had longed to follow them into medicine — then quickly denied that our thriving music trade had stood in his way. He always could comfort his mother with a hug and a kiss and a vow that he loved our life together. "I wouldn't change a thing," he'd assure me. When his eyes sometimes told me otherwise, I would push aside my whisperings of guilt. I don't think I held him back. Wouldn't he have said so?

He was well on his way to manhood those last days in Iron River, and with the death of his "Daddy Frank" he became an adult overnight. He may have been in the 8th grade, but from fourteen on he was in every way a grown man. His formal schooling ended, but he never stopped studying. He could have aimed at medicine when we first went to Chicago. Our first little apartment was near Rush Medical, and our roomers were students there. Instead, in those difficult years, studying at night, he went after civil engineering. When illness kept him from night school, he started with a correspondence school and became a certified "Junior" civil engineer, passing with honors when he was only sixteen. I was terribly proud of him.

He was always my companion and we always shared a perfect understanding. I can never forget how he cared for his mother all through our years of struggle in Chicago. I'd be away from home evening after evening giving my little recitals, but I never found him in bed upon my return. He might have dozed off, but he would be sitting up, waiting for me. In spite of hard work all day and hard study every night, he'd always set out something for me to eat — a sandwich or a custard, with everything in readiness to make mother a cup of hot coffee as soon as she came in. Early in their marriage Betty said she was surprised he knew how to cook. He bragged he'd learned how so he could help his mother. (I don't suppose she was pleased to hear that.) Frederic even tried to learn to iron, but I caught him at it one day and told him I was the only one who would wash and iron his things. It was one way I could feel close to him.

I never told Frederic his father was not Edward Smith. My son's name remained Frederic Jacobs Smith, even after I divorced Mr. Smith and married Frank Bond. Frank wanted to adopt Frederic and change his name, but Edward refused to allow it. I think my mother sensed the truth about it all, and Edward Smith probably had his suspicions. A pall of mistrust and aversion clouded our eight-year marriage almost from the beginning. I've always been glad that Frederic grew up resembling neither Dr. Bond nor Mr. Smith. He took after my mother's side of the family completely. He had Grandfather Davis's hairline and chin, and the hands and eyes of the Jacobs family. He was born on the 23rd of July, 1881. Mr. Smith and I were married on Christmas Day the year before. Count the months between and you'll understand we were the talk of Janesville for a few weeks, but not for long. Lots of seven-month babies were born in those days. People gossiped for a while, winked an eye, and went on with life. It was a time and place that faced hardship and death every day of the world, and every new baby was a blessing.

Frank Bond's father, Dr. D.W. Bond, was an uninvited observer of Frederic's birth that steamy July evening. It took place in the narrow hotel room at the Davis House where I had spent most of the years since my father's death and my mother's remarriage. Grandfather's wife Minnie was there with me. Janesville's beloved midwife Auntie Mamma had passed away, replaced by a Mrs. Flannery, a dour but altogether capable midwife. I didn't have a difficult time, but I was in added pain from the inflamed scar tissue on my back and shoulders, borne since childhood. To this day I cannot lie on my back more than a few minutes at a time. I remember that Mrs. Flannery had summoned her daughter Helen, whom she was training in the profession. We were not in a crisis of any sort, so were quite surprised when Doctor D.W. rushed in. He claimed he just happened to be in Janesville on business and heard I was in labor, but I think he sensed the truth and planned somehow to be present at the delivery of his grandchild — Frank's son Frederic "Bond." But he dutifully signed the Rock County birth certificate for Frederic Jacobs Smith.

The child that entered my life that summer was seven pounds of very active boy. He was healthy enough, except for the colic — which we were told was quite common. Maybe I was wrong. Maybe the little fellow had sensed the growing tensions between his mother and father, and sent them to his tummy. Stomach trouble plagued him all his life. Some weeks after his death I discreetly asked my dear Dr. Marshall about it. He knew Frederic's surgeon, Dr. Stein, and they had discussed his case often toward the end.

"He died of cancer, Mrs. Bond," he told me, "but they didn't know for sure until the autopsy. You'll recall he was hospitalized a few weeks before with appendicitis, and there were similar symptoms." As he spoke I recalled the closing months of his life. He (and Betty) had built a distance between us. Now I had to wonder whether it was to spare me knowledge of his pain, or to deprive him of my love and service when he knew death was coming. Either reason is heart-breaking. Dr. Marshall went on. "Had you known that Frederic was also losing his sight?" I had not, and was hurt that I'd been unable to help him through the fear he must have endured with that. I was hurt all the more that he had refrained from sharing this, too, with his mother.

I thought my last tears had been shed by this time, but I was wrong.

Dr. Marshall took my hand. "Mrs. Bond," he said, "whatever illness and pain, whatever fears about what lay ahead, whatever reverses in business Frederic was facing, they created in him an overpowering depression. I wish we could cure that with medicine or surgery. We can't."

I was sobbing. "Could I have saved him? Did I fail him somehow?"

"You've been blaming yourself ever since, haven't you, Mrs. Bond?" I couldn't speak. That blessed man took both my hands in his, tightly, as I had seen Frank Bond do with desperate patients so many years before. "Carrie Jacobs-Bond, you are one of the strongest human beings I've ever treated. You have fought down your own illnesses and your own demons, and you are alive and healthy, and you just passed your sixty-fifth birthday."

It seemed almost as if I were held once again in Frank's perfect hands. I was quieted. Then Dr. Marshall became stern, like Father had so many years ago, after my accident. "Get up out of bed, Carrie," he said. "Pull up the shades. Scrub the floors. Buy a bottle of good wine and tell your friends dinner's ready. Sing them a new song. And for God's sake, stop talking about trying to reach Frederic's spirit. He's gone. *Mrs. Bond,*" he was almost shouting, "*Get back to work.*"

So again, my life was brightened, touched by a man of medicine. I was old enough to be Dr. Marshall's mother, but in that moment he became all the beloved physicians of my life — grouchy old D.W. Bond, my husband, Frank Bond, my father, Dr. Hannibal Jacobs. I remembered Father's long-ago voice as I left that office, my tears dried and my heart pounding.

"Carrie Minetta Jacobs! Sit up straight and play!

CHAPTER 24

SEEKING FREDERIC'S SPIRIT

And thus I face the setting sun
The same sun that rose for over eighty years
To give to me a new and perfect day
To mar or beautify.
At last the sunset beckons me
With rays of brilliant light.
A gorgeous sunset marking out
A path of gold that leads me home.

So shed no tears over the sunshine of my death.
To live is wonderful,
To die is glorious,
And then the full moon silvering my journey's end.

I wrote that verse three years ago and set it aside. I return to it here, realizing that it captures in a few words the boundless grace that Frederic's death brought, after heart-breaking struggle, to my remaining years. I feel obliged to share with you, first, the agony of my search for his spirit, and then the discovery of spiritual certainly the search provided me.

I think of myself as a religious person. I was raised in the Episcopal Church. I pray every day. But I hadn't been inside a church for years until the day of Frederic's funeral. I have never found comfort in the clichés we insist on pronouncing at the grave. I'm an old lady who's been to dozens of funerals, and I'm never convinced my friends have "gone to a better world." I could not endure "God wanted him." No, not Frederic. Not yet. Not so soon. The clergy never fail to drag in the Book of Job: "The Lord giveth and the Lord hath taken away; blessed be the name of the Lord." I didn't bless the Lord, I damned Him for taking my boy. I couldn't have gotten through the service without dear friends literally holding me up — May Robson, Charlie Cadman, Mary Pickford. I was utterly disabled.

Esther Fairbanks and Betty Smith had made all the arrangements. The priest was a stranger to me, and I had to go back and look up his name before I could write this. The Reverend Father Robert Lindsey was a nice enough young man, and he called on me several times in the months that followed. At first I refused to see him, and when I finally did, try as he would, he could not convince me of "God's Grace." I suppose I was quite mean.

"You can't really help me with this, can you?" I said. "I find no comfort. Where is he? I feel his presence here, in this room, every day. We're supposed to believe life goes on — somewhere—after death, aren't we, Father Lindsey?"

He was very sweet and soft-spoken. "Why, yes, of course, Mrs. Bond," he said, "It gives us great comfort, doesn't it? We can only keep our faith that Frederic has gone to God. I do hope you believe one day you will join him there."

I said I had no such idea, that I wanted my son now. I know I shocked him when I asked, "Do you believe it's possible, somehow, to communicate with his spirit?" Poor man, he said something like, "Now, now, Mrs. Bond, you mustn't let your grief overcome your sense of reason. In prayer I'm sure you will eventually find peace." We exchanged a strained good-bye.

I do believe there was a small miracle the very next day. Grace Boylan was at my door, standing in the sunshine, with flowers and food and a box of chocolates. You'll remember I met Grace Duffie Boylan in Chicago when my new friend from the *Herald*, Amber Holden, took me to the Bohemian Club. That's the wonderful night in 1893 when I met Opie Read and Peter Dunne and Ethelbert Nevin and so many others. Grace and I became lasting friends and our paths crossed often over the years. I was proud to watch her become a well-known writer. Her books for children brought one success after another. Like so many of us she moved to California for her health — to Pasadena — where she died in 1935.

In the midst of the Great War, Grace was the anonymous author of a small book that transfixed America. As deaths on the battlefield mounted, it offered hope for grieving mothers. The first edition in 1918 was called *Messages from a Soldier to His Mother*, published in Boston by Little, Brown & Co. I had read it, not aware that dear Grace was its author. It told a story that was hard to believe, but impossible to put down. A mother tells us of the death of her son in the trenches.

Her only child, "Bob," as a boy had become obsessed with the wireless — so new and miraculous in those days. He learned the Morse Code — "dits and dots," as they used to say. Many young people were caught up in it. Frederic had puttered with it, but never really mastered the code. I found it fascinating that this mother's love for her boy inspired her to learn the wireless code right along with him. When he went off to college, they had communicated this way every night. Then came the war. Her boy was killed in France. Her wireless tapped out, *from him*, a message of his death moments after it occurred. It was several days before the army officers told her of it. In the Foreword for the first printing, the editors said:

> This manuscript was received from an author known to them, accompanied by the following letter: "The notes for this manuscript came into my possession several months ago, but I have not seen my way clear to submit it for publication until now, when the poignant grief of the world moves every heart to offer all it may of comfort. I am convinced that the simply- presented letters of the soldier killed in Flanders contain comfort for all who now mourn or must mourn in the future…I

> ask you to regard the book as truth, unaccompanied by proofs of any sort..."

Of course it's hard to believe. I shan't try to convince you of its authenticity. I did not lose my son in the war. But I'm sure my loss ten years later was as profound as that of any mother who lost a son in France. I'd like to quote a dozen more pages here, but I can tell you the dead soldier's repeated plea. Rather than to reveal insights into "the other side," his concern was for us, the living.

> There is no death. Life goes on without hindrance or handicap. The one thing that troubles the men who come here is the fact that the ones they love are in agony...Mother, be game. I am alive and loving you. But my body is with thousands of other mother's boys...Get this fact to others if you can. It's awful for us when you grieve and we can't get in touch with you and tell you we are all right...Beg the mourners to stop crying and to cease wearing black clothes.

I recall reading this in 1918. I'm not sure I believed it, but I wanted to. Any news of the dead and wounded reminded me of how mixed were my own feelings of pride and guilt. Pride, because the war had made my song *The End of a Perfect Day* popular all over the world; guilt, because Bond & Son had made huge profits. Sometime after the war, the book came out again under the title *Thy Son Liveth.* Grace Duffy Boylan was revealed as the authoress. Along with her other gifts Grace handed me a new copy that day. I saw the title and knew instantly why she had come.

I managed to make us tea. Grace scolded me for not eating as I should since Frederic's death, and insisted we have something first. Then she opened the copy of *Thy Son Liveth.* First, she dealt with the mistaken notion that it was about her own son. "I knew that, Grace," I said. "You've forgotten I've met your Malcolm. He's in the picture business right here in Hollywood." And I remembered, too, that he was her only son. Grace had inspired enough pep in me to get up and go to my cabinets and dig out a copy of *The Bird Song.* It brought us both to tears — tears of joy, and remembrance. She had written the poem and I had set it to music back in 1899. It was a lullaby we wrote for her little boy when he was two years old. I went to the piano, and we sang a stanza together:

If I could shield you from all care,
And keep your face forever fair,
As now I see it while you sleep,
These eyes of mine no more would weep,
This heart of mine its peace would keep.

The tears came again. The song brought me right back to Frederic. And Grace went to the point, the reason for her visit. "Carrie, I have never publicly identified the mother in *Thy Son Liveth*, and I never shall. But I knew her intimately, and I know her story was true. Her son communicated with her after his death!"

Grace Duffie Boylan was not a dilettante and certainly not one to be careless with the facts. When I met her in 1895, she was already a person to be reckoned with in Chicago's hard-boiled newspaper game. This was no amateur writing "The Woman's Corner" or some such trivia. Grace was an honest-to-God working reporter.

I was shaken. "Grace, what are you suggesting?"

"Let me ask you," she replied. "Have you tried to reach Frederic? In any way?"

I didn't want this question, was frightened by it. She went on. "Has he tried to communicate with you? You say you 'feel' him here. How? What do you mean?"

I had told no one, but there had been something. It had brought on a new round of sleepless nights. Some weeks after Frederic's death, I awoke one morning to find, there on the nightstand by my bed, his old Hamilton pocket watch. It had been passed down through three generations — his grandfather, then to my beloved Frank Bond, and then to 14-year-old Frederic, when Frank lay dying that dreadful December of 1895. It was a fine watch, a thing of pride to own. Two years later when Frederic went to work for the Burlington Railroad to help us through our penny-pinching Chicago years, he said he got on right away with the older men because he owned the best "railroad watch" money could buy. It was gold-plated, with initials engraved on the back — FLB — for my darling Frank Lewis Bond, Frederic's father.

That watch lived in Frederic's vest pocket for years — the hard Chicago years and the good ones, when Bond & Son was finally making money and Frederic was the manager, the accountant, the salesman. He finally put it aside when he got his commission during the war. All the officers had taken to wrist watches. Maybe you remember how first they were thought to be "feminist" or something, but then the war made them suddenly in style for men. Frederic bought one — an expensive new Hamilton of course. But he kept that railroad watch, "in safe keeping," as he said. "Who knows, Mother? Maybe pocket watches will come back in style. Some day I might have a son who'll want it."

I'd no idea where he had kept the watch. He and Betty moved half-a-dozen times. He may have left it in the Chicago office, their place in Brentwood, someplace. I hadn't seen it in over fifteen years. But there it was on the night stand, by my bed, weeks after he died. I told no one. I wrestled with my own senses, denying it was actually there, then providing myself with one theory after another for why it was perfectly logical for it to be there. I was afraid to touch it. It was still on the nightstand when I led Grace into the bedroom.

"This is Frederic's old pocket watch, Grace. I found it here one morning, a few days after his death."

She studied it. She reached over to pick it up, but I stopped her. "Was this in his vest when they found him?" she asked. "Mercy, no," I said. "He hadn't used it since the war. But it was a keepsake. For years it was almost a part of him."

Both silent, we went back into the sun room. "Carrie," Grace whispered, "he's been here. Of all the signals he could have sent, this would be his wisest choice. It speaks of his childhood, his years with you and Frank. It kept time for him through the hard years and the good years with Bond and Son. His message is simple. It explains itself."

I was weeping. "Then for God's sake, Grace, explain it *to me.* I don't understand."

"He's saying he's all right. He's urging you not to grieve. He knows your agony. In this small but unmistakable way, he's offering you release. Otherwise, as the mother said in *Thy Son Liveth,* 'a woman mourning for her son cannot be comforted.'"

Grace put her arms around me. In her warmth and wisdom I felt for the first time I could go on with my life. I slept twelve hours that night, and first thing next day, I picked up the watch and held it in my hands for a few moments, then put it away in a drawer with Frederic's letters and snapshots.

Grace had promised to come back first thing the next morning and sure enough, there she was again in the California sunshine with a basket of fruit and a fresh coffee cake. She had lots to say.

"Do you know of the author, Stewart White? The naturalist?"

I knew his work. And I had met him once, through my friend Luther Burbank. "He lives up in Santa Barbara, doesn't he?"

"He used to. They're now in a little town near San Francisco," she said. "He teaches at Stanford, I think. No matter." Grace went on to say she'd met Mr. White through his wife, Betty.

Much of what I'm going to tell you now was documented in two books the Whites published in 1937. But Grace had known years before about the remarkable events that had entered Betty's life, unannounced. She was a very practical, educated woman with no previous interest in any kind of spiritual search. Without intention she came to find herself in touch with what she called "the invisibles," anonymous entities with whom she could communicate through automatic writing, while in a trance. Grace went on to say that Stewart White fully supported Betty and helped her transcribe her revelations. Down-to-earth, scientifically-minded people, the Whites were of unquestioned integrity. Who would believe the Whites, of all people, would find themselves dealing with this phenomenon? And who, in turn, would question their honesty?

In the months that followed Grace's first visit, she and I traveled to San Francisco half-a-dozen times to see Betty and Mr. White. Please understand. Betty did not call herself a "medium." She never claimed she could communicate with the dead. But in trances, which continued until her death in 1937, she saw into planes of existence that follow human death. Her revelations confirmed the "Voice" in *Thy Son Liveth.* As I would discover, they were also confirmed by many others in the exploration of these matters over the last century. I've since read Mr. White's fascinating account of all this, and I recommend his books to you.

What I learned, and what I now carry with me in joyous anticipation, is that we are led gently at the moment of death into another stage, much the same "person" as we were the moment before. Betty's accounts, like those of so many others, are not "answers." Our existence continues to be incomplete and mysterious. It is not Heaven. It is not perfection — far from it. We step into another state of consciousness — one of a number of steps upward into increasingly wondrous states, but with no end in sight.

It took me months to examine, much less accept this radical view of death. I sought help, meanwhile, from mediums, and for a long time refused to give up hope of communicating that way with Frederic. Grace, from the start, advised me against this. Every time I told her I'd found another savant who promised success — and believe me there are lots of them in Los Angeles — she reminded me of the passage in *Thy Son Liveth:*

> Don't go to mediums. Some are, of course, genuine. But the dollar sign is to cover fraud. If you want to get in touch with us — get in touch. That is, get into a quiet corner and listen with your inner ear...You will be able to really hear what I am saying, after some practice.

I tried to do that. I tried desperately. And I read everything I could get my hands on — sometimes with Grace's help, sometimes in my own relentless search — other voices, other authorities. I talked to Gladys Leonard even before her book *My Life in Two Worlds* came out. I read the others: George Lawton, Anne Manning Roberts, George Duncan. It became an obsession — an obsession Grace endured patiently with me.

Besides Grace, my other friend and counselor was Hamlin Garland. How I miss him! I had met him in Chicago through Grace and others in that brilliant literary crowd. It was fun to discover we were both born and raised in small Wisconsin towns, he from West Salem, just two years before I was born in Janesville. Over the years I had watched his rising star as a novelist and a biographer, with a Pulitzer Prize in 1922. We became fast friends after he moved here to Hollywood in 1929, just a few months after Frederic's death. By then he had also become an authority on psychic research, a life-long interest. You can understand what brought us together.

He was such a kind, resourceful man. He and Grace brought me out of my valley of death. And here I am, a survivor, writing down my life again after 83 years on earth. I am unashamed to tell you that yes, I had considered taking my own life many times after Frederic died. And I was sure that if I couldn't bring myself to it, grief would eventually kill me. But after my year of searching and seclusion, I found Carrie Jacobs-Bond was still there, the one I knew before the black day in 1928. I traveled again, made new friends, wrote new songs, started a new career on the radio.

People said how can you go on? I believe Frederic's widow Betty actually held it against me that I could and did go on. My year of grief became also a year of seeking, of breaking through old beliefs and finding comfort in new ones. The result of my utter failure to communicate with Frederic led me to truths that I believe will inform my own death. The depth of my study of what the world calls psychic phenomena or spiritualism has brought to me a belief I would never have dreamed possible. I want to share this belief with you. I've gone over it many times with my editor, Rose Ives, to find just the right words. Here are the points — the *truths* — we finally agreed upon:

Two-way communication with those we pronounce "dead" is not possible. But they, in ways and forms beyond our imagination, can reveal themselves to us. I fully believe the mother's story in *Thy Son Liveth.*

> The human spirit or essence survives the death of the earthly body. The evolution of humanity continues, within a universe of infinite time and unimaginable nature.
>
> Knowledge of these phenomena, now considered pseudo-scientific, will eventually submit to scientific proof.
>
> Finally, this conclusion, which will be upsetting to many of you (but not to me): none of this has to do with God. Accepting these discoveries as truth, however, should not interfere with or hinder one's hope for a Supreme Being. That search continues.

Except for the pocket watch, I never heard from Frederic again, and was finally reconciled to his death. One of the mediums I consulted stunned me by saying that suicide cuts forever the spirit's access to the next plane. I chose not to believe him. My search convinces me that the sins and the misfortunes and the traps of earthly life do not follow us. We are not punished. And the death of the lowliest "savage" is the same as the death of the most learned and civilized. There are no favorites. Grace and I agreed this might be an intimation of what we call God's mercy. I brought to her attention that the young man in *Thy Son Liveth*, reported that the "despised Huns" could not make the crossing with "our boys." Rubbish, we agreed. That was simply evidence that our crossing into "death" is not an assurance of perfect knowledge and enlightenment.

I am not obsessed by these revelations. They rest comfortably in the back of my mind as I move thankfully through my last years on earth. I have continued further reading from time to time, especially the work of the great British psychologist and scholar Frederic Myers. (He also spelled his Frederic without the "k," like mine.) He saw through all the easy tricks and deceptions of fake spiritualism, but was convinced after years of research that the soul progresses through those after-death states. One of his colleagues wrote that he "never knew a man so hopeful concerning his ultimate destiny." Perhaps my Frederic's death was meant to lead me here as well, to this peaceful assurance. At the end of his long and distinguished career, Frederic Myers was often heard to say, "I am counting the days until the holidays."

So am I.

CARRIE JACOBS-BOND

January 10, 1946

Printed in the United States
153732LV00002B/3/P

FICTION / GENERAL

I LOVE YOU TRULY is the fictionalized autobiographical tale of Carrie Jacobs-Bond, one of the most successful composers and publishers of American popular music during the twentieth century.

Carrie Jacobs-Bond was an enterprising pioneer a century ago in the infant business of Popular Music, often referred to in those days as "Tin Pan Alley." She was a tough, calculating, worldly woman of great passions who made a fortune in what was then strictly a man's world. Her life began in a frontier Wisconsin town during the Civil War and ended at age eighty-four when more than 5,000 people paid their respects at Forest Lawn cemetery in Hollywood, where the valediction was given by a former president of the United States. As composer of three of the best-known and longest-lasting love songs of her time, Jacobs-Bond's life was affectionately covered in magazines and newspapers, but she was far more than the image she had created for herself as a quiet, motherly woman who happened to write, as she often said, some "little songs."

Max Morath has enlarged upon the life of this courageous and talented woman, who was nearly forty years old before the gift of music lifted her out of poverty and transformed her into an international celebrity.

"Max Morath is a philosopher of American popular culture ... musicologist, storyteller, and expert in turn-of-the-century Americana."

—STEPHEN HOLDEN, NEW YORK TIMES

"Morath brings to everything he touches a keen intelligence and encyclopedic knowledge of every aspect, musical and otherwise, of late 19th and early 20th century Americana."

—RICHARD M. SUDHALTER, NEW YORK POST

DIANE FAY SKOMARS

MAX MORATH'S one-man shows on ragtime and musical theater have tallied over five thousand performances in sixty-odd years of touring. His recordings for Vanguard and RCA and his pioneering productions for PBS are considered classics. He's the author of The Road to Ragtime and The NPR Curious Listener's Guide to Popular Standards.

$13.95

www.iuniverse.com